CAMERON 3

A NOVEL BY

JADE JONES

www.jadedpub.com

This novel is a work of fiction. Any reference to real people, events, establishments, or locales is intended only to give the fiction a sense of reality and authenticity. Other names, characters, and incidents occurring in the work are either the product of the author's imagination or are used fictitiously, as are those fictionalized events and events that involve real persons. Any character that happens to share the name of a person who is any acquaintance of the author, past or present, is purely coincidental and is in no way intended to be an actual account involving that person.

1

Sitting on top of the closed toilet seat lid in her master bathroom, Cameron stared at the positive pregnancy test that she had taken less than five minutes ago. Her vision blurred as tears slowly formed in her almond shaped eyes.

Sighing dejectedly, Cameron ran her fingers through her natural brown shoulder length hair and stared at the dark blue line indicating positive. It seemed as if her entire world was crashing down around her.

Damn.

Suddenly, Cameron's cell phone began vibrating on the bathroom counter sink. The annoying buzzing sound interrupted her thoughts and contemplation about the dreaded future. She blew out air at the sight of the caller ID, and started not to even answer. After all, she didn't even know what to say.

Against Cameron's better judgment, she answered on the fifth ring. "Hello?" she breathed into the mouthpiece.

"Look, you ain't gotta talk, Cameron" Marcus said. "Just listen...I know you gotta man and everything. I dig that you're faithful and shit but I can't get you out of my head. I'm really feelin' you, Cameron" he admitted. "And when that nigga fuck up, I'ma be right here waitin' on you to hopefully take a chance with me..."

Tears formed in Cameron's eyes at the mere mention of Jude. Five years felt like an eternity. *Why is all this shit happening to me*?

Suddenly, and without warning, Cameron's cell phone slipped from her trembling fingers and landed on the plush cream contour rug. Tears spilled over her lower lids and landed on her bare thighs. She could hear Marcus calling out to her in the distance, but she didn't think twice about retrieving the phone.

After all, what Cameron was feeling right now had nothing to do with him. As a matter of fact, it had nothing to do with Jude.

It was about her.

Slowly standing to her feet, Cameron gradually made my way over towards the bathroom's vanity. Once she reached the mirror, she looked over her reflection. Strangely, it felt like Cameron didn't even recognize the woman staring back at her.

Who is this stranger?

Who is this young girl staring back at me?

I don't know you.

Minutes quickly passed as Cameron stood in the mirror watching herself cry...

So many thoughts ran through her mind. Shit was too crazy lately and it was only getting crazier. The reality of it all was that Cameron was alone. Alone in this crazy ass world she called life.

Slowly, she reached for the top drawer, and pulled it open. A few seconds later, Cameron brandished a pair of sharp-edged scissors. With trembling fingers, she brought the scissors unnervingly closer to her face all the while staring directly at her reflection.

Before she could think twice about what she was doing, she began hacking off her beautiful hair...

***

"Cameron? Cameron?!" Marcus called out. He pulled his Samsung Galaxy away from his face and stared at the screen for several seconds. The call's timer was still going so it was obvious that Cameron hadn't disconnected the call. "Yo! Cameron?!"

Marcus had a half a mind to just drive over to Cameron's condo and see what was up with her. Then he remembered that tonight was The Punisher's "All White Affair Birthday Bash." Anytime any of the dancers celebrated a birthday coupled with a unique theme, there was bound to be tons of money to be made; especially considering the few dancers who were coming from out of town in order to make special guest appearances.

There was Satisfaction from ATL, Boy Toy from Memphis, and Warning coming all the way from Miami.

Marcus finally disconnected the call after it was apparent that Cameron was done with the conversation. *I don't know what this chick is on, but I hope she aight,* he thought to himself.

Marcus then scanned the time on his cellphone's home screen. It was 7:46 p.m. The doors to the show opened at 9:00 p.m., granted Marcus also needed time to briefly mingle with the crowd, prepare for his performance, and reach a certain level of high in order to feel comfortable enough to perform.

Marcus was by no means a man with low self-esteem. With smooth dark chocolate skin, a low haircut with soft brush waves, and a neatly trimmed goatee, Marcus was often told that he resembled running back for the Miami Dolphins, Reggie Bush. He was a pretty boy with a rugged demeanor.

"You ready to roll out?" Psyklone aka Xavier asked as he took a final pull on his tightly rolled blunt. The expression he gave Marcus pretty much said it all, but he decided to hold his thoughts back. *Why is he sweating this bitch like he can't have whatever girl he wants*?

Marcus was no fool, and didn't miss the look in his homie's eyes. "Lemme hit that shit real quick," he said walking over towards Xavier who sat comfortably on Marcus's smoky Glencrest sofa.

Xavier handed over the blunt, stood to his feet and stretched. He was six feet three inches tall, possessed the body of a Greek God, and was considerably handsome with his chiseled facial features and smooth brown skin. His shoulder length dreadlocks were always tied back, and a mural of tattoos adorned his body from the neck down. An ex-drug dealer turned exotic dancer, Xavier was practically born with a hustler's instinct.

"I mean it ain't my business but—"

"So why you in mine?" Marcus cut Xavier off before taking an aggressive drag on the blunt.

"Bruh, this bitch got a..." His voice immediately trailed off the minute Marcus cut his eyes at him. Instead of initiating a confrontation, Xavier decided to drop the subject...for now.

Marcus and Xavier had been longtime friends ever since they each got involved in the male exotic dancing business. Xavier, by no means, hated on his homeboy's feelings toward Cameron, but he just knew that Cameron also came with a load of baggage via the streets. Her ex-boyfriend, Silk had committed suicide, and her best friend Pocahontas had gotten murked by some random cat in the streets. Xavier would just hate to see his boy, Marcus fall prey to Cameron's never-ending drama.

***

Cameron stared at her reflection in the bathroom mirror. She now looked like a cross between Britney Spears and Miley Cyrus after they hacked off their precious hair. She now felt a whole lot better, but unfortunately her appearance didn't match the way she felt.

Cameron's eyes slowly wandered down towards the mess she had made in the sink. She looked at her hair, and considered it to be the past and pain she had experienced over the months.

"What did you do girl?" she asked herself.

Her bizarre appearance was actually kind of amusing. Now she had to think of a stylish way she would have to wear her butchered hair.

Suddenly, and without warning, vomit shot up from the pit of her stomach. She rushed towards the porcelain toilet, and before she could kneel down in front of it, the contents of her stomach sprayed onto the toilet seat and plush contour rug beneath her feet.

Cameron dropped to her knees, landing in the small puddle of vomit, and puked into the toilet bowl for what felt like hours until she was spitting up nothing more than yellowish stomach acid. Painful spasms followed shortly after.

After wiping away the lengthy dribble of drool oozing off her bottom lip, Cameron gently laid her head against the rim of the toilet. She slowly closed her eyes and contemplated what she was going to do about her unexpected pregnancy. Cameron didn't know the first thing about raising a child, and she surely didn't sign up for the stressful position of being a single parent with Jude behind bars.

***

DJ won't you play this girl a love song...

She really needs to hear this freakin' love song...

She's lookin' at me kinda hard, I can tell that things ain't right on the home front...

What she really needs is a G like me to beat a beat, beat it, beat it...

Peer Pressure serenaded across the stage of Pandora's Box as he enticed the female audience with his X-Rated performance. A pair of unbuttoned, unzipped, loose fitting denim jeans hung off his waist. Oil glistened on his smooth chestnut colored skin, and his body was toned and ripped to perfection.

Peer Pressure was the youngest male dancer employed at Pandora's Box at only twenty-two years old, but his popularity outweighed some of the vets who had been in the business for years.

Women hooted and hollered from the audience as if they were at a Trey Songz concert instead of a male revue birthday bash. Flashing bills in their hands, and wide grins on their faces it was obvious that everyone was there for unadulterated entertainment at its finest.

Gotcha wanna try me...

Homeboy can't please ya...

On this wall in the open baby...

You wouldn't care if the crowd was watchin' baby...

You want it...

I know it...

Gotta notion to pull yo' ass up outta here...

Marcus aka Klimaxxx swaggered through the thick crowd of onlookers making sure to stop at every table in the club in order to greet and/or introduce himself to the guests. He wanted to make sure the women had a good look at him before he went on stage to do his thing. Mingling with the audience before his performance always ensured that he'd get tipped well.

Marcus loved the overwhelming attention he received from the many women doing what he did. He wore a pair of high top sneakers, khakis, and a $230 designer t-shirt by Maison Martin Margiela. Marcus lifted his shirt up, and allowed women to rub and caress his rock hard six pack as they admired his toned physique.

Any man would argue that this was the life, and Marcus honestly had no real issue with the money he earned, but he would be damned if he did this shit forever. He had long-term goals and dreams that went far beyond taking his clothes off, and shaking his dick for money. Dancing was only something temporary for him.

"Oh my God! His abs is so freaking hard!" One of Marcus's admirers exclaimed as she gently ran her slender fingers over his abdomen where the word: *Klimaxxx* was tattooed in bold Old English text.

She looked no older than twenty-three or twenty-four years old, was brown-skinned and rather slender in frame. A pair of black Burberry eyeglasses rested on her narrow nose and she was cute in a nerdy, innocent sense.

"This ain't the only thing that's hard, baby," Marcus flirted.

The young female's eye shot open in disbelief after his comment. She offered a girlish giggle in response.

Xavier suddenly walked up to Marcus and tapped him on his shoulder. "I'm up after Peer Pressure and then it's on you," he told him before walking off.

Marcus nodded his head, bent down towards his nerdy admirer, and whispered something in her ear. A smile tugged at the corner of her lips as she nodded her head. Marcus then made his way towards the dressing room in order to prepare for his performance.

Once inside Marcus took a seat at the vanity and pulled out his cellphone to see if Cameron had called. He was the only one inside the dressing room since all the other dancers were on the floor mingling. As expected, he received no call or text message from her.

"Damn. What's up with her?" Marcus ran a hand over his soft brush waves in frustration.

It was crazy how a woman could have so much influence over his life that had done nothing even remotely significant for him. Hell, Marcus and Cameron had never even slept with one another and there he was sweating her like a nerdy teen in high school crushing on the most popular cheerleader. Marcus couldn't get the chick off his mind, and he was far from being pressed for pussy especially considering his profession.

Women practically threw themselves at him. Male strippers got as much love and attention as a professional athlete or popular music artist. As fucked up as it sounded women were at his disposal, so Marcus couldn't, for the life of him figure out why he was sweating Cameron so hard.

It's just something about her, he continued to tell himself over and over. *It's always just been something about her*.

Even when Cameron used to date his deceased homeboy Silk, Marcus constantly found his eyes straying to Cameron's luscious body, smooth pecan colored skin, and gorgeous smile. She was bad as hell and she knew it, and so did everyone else who laid eyes on her.

What he was feeling most of all about Cameron was that she had goals in life. He was digging the fact that she was in college, and actually pursuing something. There was nothing worse than a bitch without goals or expectations in life.

Marcus tried to shake Cameron from his thoughts as he refocused on the money that needed to be made tonight. Pulling out a tiny plastic baggie from his jeans pocket, he examined the colorful miniscule pills inside. This was his addiction, and seemingly he needed it just to feel comfortable enough to perform.

Marcus abided by the same routine for the few years he had been entertaining. He quickly undressed, popped two ecstasy pills, and slowly waited for the wonderful high to come soon after. He had tried on several occasions to quit popping, but he just couldn't kick the addiction no matter how hard he tried. After pulling on a pair of olive camo cargo shorts, and black combat boots, he topped the outfit off with a vintage army fatigue hat.

Knock!

Knock!

Marcus averted his attention to the soft taps on the dressing room's door. He knew who was on the opposite end, before the door even opened seconds after. Marcus's nerdy admirer traipsed into the dressing room with a Cheshire cat grin on her pretty face.

Marcus didn't even know her name nor did he care to. He was just happy that she had actually come.

"You wanted me to meet you back here?" she asked breathlessly. She felt a combination of nervousness and anxiousness.

She knew she had no business being back there alone with Marcus especially since she had a man who would literally break her little ass in half if he even knew where she was. However, she had allowed her girls to peer pressure her into attending the show. She promised herself that she would at least behave herself, but the minute Marcus had whispered in her ear to meet him in the dressing room in twenty minutes, she had tossed her promise out the window—as well as the fact that she had a fiancée. A few shots of Grey Goose in her system had her thinking and preparing to behave irrationally.

Marcus grinned, and held up a small bottle of baby oil. "Rub me down real quick..." It was more a statement than an actual question.

His nerdy admire slowly made her way over towards him. Her clit began to throb at the mouthwatering sight of Marcus. His defined, muscular torso beckoned for her hands to touch and caress him all over. She slowly took the bottle from Marcus and proceeded to oil his toned upper back. Once his back was oiled to perfection she lathered his chest and abdomen down.

"That's good?" she asked revealing that wide grin of hers.

Marcus could hear Twista's *"Get It Wet"* in the distance. He wondered if Xavier was up on stage by now.

He took a seat in the chair and pulled his admirer into his lap. "You know you sexy as fuck in a librarian kinda way," he told her.

She giggled and looked away.

"You gotta man?" Marcus asked.

She looked down and nodded her head.

Marcus didn't give a damn as he guided her hand towards his crotch and placed her small palm over it. Her eyes instantly bulged in their sockets as she allowed him to ease her hand up and down his lengthy dick through his cargo shorts.

This wasn't initially part of his plan, and Marcus usually wasn't this mannish and impulsive, but he was feeling the effects of the ecstasy he had popped. He slowly removed her eyeglasses and placed them on the vanity's countertop.

"You pretty as fuck," Marcus said telling her exactly what she wanted to hear. "You gon' tip me when I go up on stage right?" he asked.

She nodded her head eagerly. "Of course," she answered. "I'ma tell my girls to too."

That's exactly what he wanted to hear.

"I appreciate it...with your fine ass."

She smiled bashfully.

He slowly leaned in, and placed a peck on her small lips. She responded by trying to slide her tongue in his mouth, but he quickly pulled away. He wasn't trying to do all that extra shit.

"Why don't you suck it for me a little bit," he offered.

A respectable chick would have asked him if he were crazy, slapped the hell out of him, and left the dressing room, but his nerdy admirer surprised him when she slid down onto her knees, pulled his thick dick out, and obliged his offer.

Marcus reclined his head, closed his eyes, and groaned softly as she went to work. Her looks were definitely deceiving because she seemingly sucked him off better than Karrine Steffan's legendary head game.

Her head bobbed up and down in his lap as she made sloppy gagging sounds, and Marcus loved every minute of the shit. He placed his hand on the back of her head, and envisioned her soft lips as Cameron's as she polished his dick. He could just imagine how wet and warm Cameron's mouth would feel wrapped around his hard dick.

"Damn, that shit feels so good," Marcus moaned. "Don't stop..."

"Aye bruh, you up!" Xavier said busting inside the dressing room with his bare dick swinging for the world to see. He wasn't surprised to find some random chick sucking Marcus off, because that was something the male dancers saw on the regular. "Fans" as they often referred to as their loyal customers, went hard for them. Plain and simple. It was just the way shit went.

Marcus's female friend instantly jumped up at the sound of Xavier's voice. She had gone from freaked out to ashamed in a matter of seconds. Quickly standing to her feet, she snatched her glasses off the countertop, and crookedly placed them on her face before scurrying out of the dressing room in embarrassment.

"Damn," Xavier laughed shaking his head in amusement. "The hell was up with her? Anyway watch table four," he warned his friend. "It's a bunch of fat ass bitches that wanna grope all day, but ain't got no money to pay."

"Good looking," Marcus said as he fixed up his clothing and prepared to make his way out into the club.

Pretty Willie's "*Lay Your Body Down*" played on maximum as he made his way into the dimly lit crowded club. Colorful strobe lights reflected off his oily muscular chest, and the women were hollering and screaming like Lil' Wayne had just stepped into the building.

In the farthest corner of the room, Marcus spotted a woman that he had dated periodically throughout his life. They had never been in a full blown relationship, but he did develop feelings for her over time and vice versa. She was a "get money" type of broad, and the chicks sitting at the table with her looked like they were too so he sensuously danced his way over towards her table.

Pure Seduction bit her bottom lip seductively as Marcus eased her chair closer to him and danced in front of her. "Is that dick still as good as I remember?" she boldly asked.

Marcus leaned down towards her ear and flicked his tongue over her earlobe. "It's gotten even better," he whispered.

2

After a grueling two hours of processing, Cameron was finally permitted inside the prison visitation room. Luckily Jude was in the general population so he was able to have contact visits. It was already hard enough for the couple to deal with Jude's lengthy imprisonment, and not being able to have physical contact would crush them.

Cameron slowly ambled towards the table where Jude sat with his hands clasped together in front of him, and a half smile on his face. He wore a tan prison jumpsuit, and looked rather weary and stressed, but he tried to push his issues and worries to the back of his mind for the sake of seeing his woman.

Cameron's smug expression didn't hide the way she felt. She obviously had some things on her mind. Dressed in a vintage Vans sweater, loose fitting denim jeans, and a pair of black Jordans without an ounce of makeup on her face, Jude automatically knew something was up with his girl because she usually dressed up where ever she went. His eyes then wandered to the Rihanna inspired haircut she was now rocking.

The new haircut actually suited her quite well, but Jude would be lying if he said he didn't love the shoulder length bob that Cameron was accustomed to wearing.

Jude quickly stood to his feet once Cameron reached his table. They embraced each other and Jude held on tighter as they hugged. He kissed her forehead, and then placed a brief kiss on her dry lips. Contact was limited, and the correctional officers were known for tripping on inmates if they got a little too touchy.

Cameron and Jude then took their seats across from one another. Jude noticed Cameron's dry demeanor immediately. As a matter of fact, she wasn't even looking at him. Instead she was eyeing an inmate visiting his wife and four year old son.

Jude decided to initiate the conversation. "I see you cut your hair," he said.

Cameron slowly peeled her gaze away from the inmate to look at her man. Just as handsome and calm as the day he was when she met him for the first time in Columbus, she was just as attracted to him now as she was back then. It was just fucked up how unfortunate circumstances had gotten in the way of their once perfect relationship.

Cameron licked her dry lips, exhaled deeply, and looked down at her hands. "Cut it last night," she said nonchalantly.

Jude nodded his head. He didn't want to question her as to why she had cut her hair off and risk the chance of upsetting her; especially since it was clear that something was on her mind.

He ran a hand through his mid-length dreadlocks. "I been missin' you," he admitted in a low tone.

Cameron didn't respond immediately and that actually hurt Jude a little. He reached over to touch her hand, but didn't miss her instantly tense up. That hurt even more. “Bay, you aight?” he finally asked. “You know if you got some shit on ya mind, you can tell me.”

Cameron looked up into Jude’s beautiful brown eyes that were complemented by long, thick eyelashes. He was sexy as he wanted to be with his smooth light skin and handsome facial features. She loved his lips most of all. They weren’t too thick, but they weren’t too small, and they were soft as hell.

Damn, Cameron thought. She loved this man in front of her with every fiber of her being, but she was unsure if she was willing and/or able to hold him down in his time of need especially when she needed him as well.

“I have something to tell you,” Cameron whispered. She was barely audible, but luckily Jude heard her so she wouldn’t have to repeat herself.

“Baby, you can tell me anything,” Jude said. And he meant that...but accepting it was a whole other story. Every night he prayed that Cameron wouldn’t give up on him, because he needed her now more than ever.

Cameron swallowed the large lump that formed in her throat, and sighed dejectedly. Jude slowly reached over and placed his hands on top of Cameron’s. She didn’t tense up that time. As a matter of fact she relaxed a little.

“I took a pregnancy test last night,” she admitted in a low tone.

Jude’s breath felt like it had caught in his chest as he waited for her to finish.

"It came back positive…" Cameron looked up from their hands to see Jude's expression.

His jaw muscle tensed, and he closed his eyes briefly as he allowed her words to sink in. Cameron took his gesture to mean that he was either upset or disappointed by the news.

"You look mad," Cameron whispered.

Jude looked over at his woman intensely. "Babe…I'm not," he paused. "I'm not upset. I'm not pissed. I'm just mad at myself," he said in a calm tone. "I'm mad at the fact that I'm sittin' my black ass in here, and I can't be there for you like a man supposed to be for his woman." He ran a hand through his dreadlocks and sighed in frustration. "It's just…it's fucked up man." He shook his head. "I just…I don't know what to do," he whispered.

"You don't have to do anything," Cameron told him. "I'll go to the clinic and make sure that I'm actually pregnant," she said. "And if I am…I plan on getting an abortion..."

Now it was Jude's turn to tense up. He quickly pulled his hands away from Cameron's and stared at her in disbelief. He had to be sure that he was hearing her correctly because he truly couldn't believe the shit coming out of her mouth.

"What'd you just say?" Jude asked in irritation. His cheeks instantly flushed in anger at the mere mention of abortion. "Yo, you're not killin' my fuckin' baby if you're pregnant—"

"You don't have a say in what the fuck I do with my body," Cameron said through gritted teeth.

Jude was taken aback by Cameron's harsh response. He wasn't used to hearing her speak this way. "You're my woman," Jude said. "And that's my baby. I think that gives me more than enough say, don't you think?"

"That doesn't matter," Cameron said as tears slowly formed in her eyes. "You're in here. I'm the one that's out there struggling to live without you. I'm in school..." She frowned and tears slowly slid down her reddened cheeks. "What the hell do you think?" Cameron asked. "I'ma be bringing the baby up here every other fucking week to see your ass? It's enough trying to take care of myself," she told Jude. "I'm not ready for any kids..."

Jude shook his head vehemently. "Cameron, God gave us this blessing a second time for a reason. I can't even believe I'm hearin' this shit right now," he said. "The reckless ass way you talkin'. You sound selfish as fuck—"

"Selfish?!" Cameron spat. "I sound like I'm thinking about what's best for both of us," she said before wiping her tears away. "You're in prison. We're not financially stable." Cameron reached over towards Jude's hands. "Bay...we're not ready..."

Jude moved his hands away from Cameron and continued to shake his head in disbelief. "You're givin' up on me," he finally said.

Cameron was clearly offended by that statement. "What do you mean I'm giving up on you?" she asked. "I'm here aren't I?"

"Yeah, but for how long?" Jude asked with a serious expression. "You're already givin' up on our unborn kid," he said. "How long before you give up on ya man? Huh?" he asked.

Cameron stared deep into Jude's eyes. She matched his intense stare with her own. "I don't know...," she said flatly.

Jude felt like he had just taken a fierce blow to the gut. Hearing her say that let him know that there was in fact a possibility of him losing her. "Cameron, don't say that shit," he pleaded shaking his head. "Don't say that..."

More tears escaped from Cameron's eyes. "You're in here, Jude—"

"Cameron, you're my woman. You're supposed to be my fuckin' rock." His voice cracked as he spoke. Jude was overwhelmed with emotions. This was Cameron's third visit since he had been imprisoned, and this visit was definitely proving to be the most intense. "I need you," he told her. "I need you in my life, babe. And if you're really pregnant...as selfish as you may think I'm being, I need that baby too," he admitted. "I need you to get me through the days in this mothafucka, bay," he told her. Tears slid down his cheeks as he spoke. "I need you just to sleep at night," he whispered. "Cameron, you don't know what the fuck I'm goin' through in here. I need you so bad...I need you baby...Don't talk to me like this. Please..." There was so much desperation and pain in Jude's eyes that Cameron was unable to meet his gaze.

He reached over to touch her hands again, but she quickly pulled them away and placed them in her lap. "I can't keep this baby Jude," she said looking down.

"Cameron—"

"I can't!" Cameron suddenly yelled. "I'm not ready for this shit! And I can't do this shit by myself!"

Jude's nostrils flared in anger as he searched Cameron's face. He barely even recognized her and it had nothing to do with her attire and new haircut.

Cameron sniffled and wiped her nose with the sleeve of her sweater. "I have a little something for you," she said before digging into the pocket of her jeans. She then pulled out a crinkled fifty dollar bill, placed it on the cold metal table, and slid it over towards Jude.

He frowned at the sight of the money not knowing what she had to do to get it. He prayed that she hadn't resorted to stripping when she promised him that she was done with it for good.

"Man, I don't want that shit," Jude told her in a nasty tone. He hated that she was trying to use money to change the subject or better yet to pacify him.

Cameron was shocked and offended by his reaction. Without another word, she grabbed the bill shoved it into her pocket, and quickly stood to her feet.

"Cameron," Jude said in a serious tone.

"I think this visit is done," she said not bothering to look at him. "And so am I."

Jude stood to his feet and placed his hands on the table. "So that's what that lil' punk ass money was about?" he asked. Cameron had never offered him any money since he had been locked up and he didn't want her to. She knew that he was far too proud to accept anything from anyone. "Huh?" he asked. "I can't fuckin' believe you." Jude's tone was laced with pain and anger. "I'm not a perfect nigga. I know I'm not. And I admit I wasn't real with you from the jump, but the love I got for you is. I went over and beyond to show you I'ma good dude, and now you turnin' yo' back on me?" he asked. "Cameron, look at me..."

Cameron forced herself to look at Jude as she blinked back tears.

"Please don't tell me fallin' in love with you a mistake," Jude said in a low tone. "Please just tell me you're scared right now..."

Cameron ran a hand over her short hair and sighed. She looked up at the ceiling, rolled her eyes, and tried to hold back the oncoming tears. "I just can't do this right now Jude...I can't—I just can't." Suddenly, Cameron turned on her heel and walked swiftly out of the visitation room.

"Cameron!" Jude called out after her. "*Cameron*!"

***

Cameron drew in a deep breath of fresh air the minute she reached the parking lot. She couldn't stand the stale scent of the prison. She couldn't stand the jumpsuits. She couldn't stand the neediness in Jude's eyes.

"Fuck," she cursed as she quickly sped walked to her Audi q7. The vehicle Jude had purchased for her. His words echoed over and over again in Cameron's mind*: I went over and beyond to show you I'ma good dude, and now you turnin' yo' back on me*?

Once Cameron reached her car, she pulled her keys out and stuck the car key into the keyhole....well actually she tried to several times, but with trembling fingers she missed the first several attempts until she got fed up, tossed the car keys, and slowly sank down onto the ground where she began to cry hysterically.

Cameron leaned against her truck and grabbed fistfuls of her short hair. "Stupid! Stupid! Stupid!" she screamed. She felt like shit about everything she had said, but unfortunately it was too late to take it back now.

3

Jude tried his best to remain strong as he made his way back to his 6x8 prison cell that he was forced to live in with another grown ass man. He felt like he was on the verge of breaking down, but the last thing Jude wanted was for his fellow inmates to see him at his weakest and possibly use it against him.

The heavy metal door to Jude's prison cell opened, and he reluctantly stepped inside. Being in prison was worse than being in hell, and Jude wouldn't wish this shit on his worst enemy. However, he firmly believed in the motto "If you do the crime, you must pay the time." And he was damn sure paying for it...physically, mentally, emotionally...hell, even socially. Prison was built to make a sane man go crazy.

The metal door slammed shut behind Jude, and he slowly took a seat on the hard circular stool that was positioned in front of the stainless steel desk bolted to the wall. He looked totally out of it as he sat still with this faraway look in his dark eyes.

His cellmate Larry sat up in bed. He resided in the bottom bunk, and he never got any visitors nor did he expect to have any anytime soon. Not for the unspeakable crime he had committed.

"You aight son," he asked in a concerned tone. Larry was fifteen years Jude's senior.

Jude suddenly flipped out. "Nigga, don't fuckin' talk to me!" he spat. "Don't look at me! Don't even acknowledge my fuckin' presence!"

Larry remained calm as he allowed Jude to blatantly disrespect him. If it was any other young punk, Larry—who was six feet five inches tall and weighed a solid two-hundred and fifty pounds—would have laid their asses out, but Jude was his cellmate and they had to be able to live and tolerate each other. Besides, Jude had never jumped crazy at him before, and Larry figured that he probably just had a bad visit.

"Okay," Larry nodded in understanding. "Okay."

Jude, who was clearly frustrated and upset, dropped down onto the cold, cement ground and began doing pushups aggressively. He couldn't believe how weak Cameron had portrayed herself to be.

***

Marcus was cruising through downtown Cleveland in his custom gunmetal black Chrysler 300. The interior was foggy as hell as he and Xavier smoked on the best loud Cleveland had to offer.

Notorious B.I.G.'s *"Nigga's Bleed"* blared through the speakers of Marcus's car as they made their way to Club Lush located off Superior Avenue.

Xavier sucked in a lungful of smoke, and suddenly went into a brief coughing fit before handing the blunt back to Marcus. "Aye, nigga, did you see the way Punisher was hatin' last night?" he asked. "Nigga was mad everybody made money *but* him on his own birthday," he chuckled.

"Fuck that nigga," Marcus chuckled before taking a pull on the blunt. "Nigga too old to be still dancin' anyway," he said. "Need to be worrying about not burstin' a blood vessel while he fuckin' with that dick pump."

Xavier and Marcus cackled at the crude thought. They doubted the women would still feel the same way about some of the male dancers who vacuumed their dicks just to be able to get hard enough to perform.

Five minutes later, they pulled into the over-capacitated parking lot of Club Lush. It was only 10:30 p.m. and already there was a line that damn near wrapped around the corner. One would've thought they were waiting in line to vote.

Marcus wasn't worried though. His days of having to wait in line or worst, being denied entrance, had long since come to an end.

After parking his car, Marcus and Xavier headed to the entry doors of the club, but not before handing out a few flyers for their next upcoming show. Women smiled, winked, and whispered in their girlfriends' ears about which brother they would love to take home and fuck, and which man they already had the pleasure of doing such a thing with. Men scoffed and hated in the distance, but that was the normal effect for both fellas.

Marcus tried to call Cameron again before he entered the noisy club to see if she was okay, but her line rang multiple times before sending him to the voicemail. Shrugging it off, he stepped into the crowded club.

***

I am smoking on that gas; life should be on Cinemax...

Movie, bought my boo bigger tits and a bigger ass...

Who he's, not I, I smoke strong, that Popeye...

Louie V's in my archives, black diamonds, apartheid!

2 Chainz and Drake's "*No Lie*" blared through the massive speakers of Club Lush. Marcus maneuvered through the thick crowd as he made his way towards Xavier who was dancing and feeling himself a little extra hard. He and Marcus were the flyest dudes in the club. Chicks were with their men, and still eyeballing the young, flashy guys.

Xavier wore a $130 black and gold Lichtenberg's Homie sweater, and a pair of designer jeans. On his size fourteen were a pair of black Chanel boots. Gold chains hung loosely around his neck, and on his wrist was a polished gold Versace watch.

Marcus looked equally as fly dressed in a limited edition Ron Bass Varsity Jacket and a 40oz NYC Snapback. On his feet was a pair of $700 Maison Martin Margiela sneakers. Before he could even make his way back to his homeboy with their beverages he was suddenly pulled by his arm. It wasn't an aggressive pull. It was actually soft and feminine if anything.

Marcus turned to face the woman who was pulling his arm. He was surprised to see the nerdy chick from Pandora's Box that had given him brain in the dressing room. She wasn't wearing her glasses tonight and she was scantily dressed in a matte mesh dress that exposed about seventy percent of her body. Marcus immediately knew the eyeglasses were a front. A sly smile tugged at her lips and he knew off rip what she was thinking.

"Klimaxxx," she smiled licking her lips. It was obvious that she was slightly intoxicated.

Marcus grimaced after she sloshed the contents of her wine glass onto his designer sneakers. "Marcus," he corrected her. "You can call me Marcus," he forced a smile. Always be cordial to the fans no matter what was his motto. He started to walk off.

She quickly grabbed his arm again stopping him from leaving. "I like calling you Klimaxx," she purred. "I was wondering when we can finish what we started last night."

Marcus's thick eyebrows furrowed in confusion. "Aye, who are you here with tonight?" he asked.

Before she could even respond, a Flo Rida look alike snatched her away from Marcus so aggressively that her neck nearly snapped. "Aye, what the fuck is you doing, Mia?!" he roared. "Bitch, you must be tryin' to get you and this corny ass nigga fucked up!" he pointed at Marcus.

Corny? *Never that,* Marcus thought.

"I wasn't doing anything, Damonte!" Mia yelled.

Instead of feeding into the drama, Marcus decided to let it go. That was their problem now his. He wasn't in the mood to crack any nigga's heads, and besides tonight was a night of celebration. Marcus headed back towards Xavier and left Mia and her man to argue with one another in the center of the dance floor.

"Took yo' ass so long?" Xavier asked relieving Marcus of one of the beers.

Marcus took a swig of his beer. Before he could even get a buzz going, two random females approached him and began dancing on him. He was having the time of his life when he noticed Damonte walk up to a few other guys. Seconds later, they were mean-mugging the hell out of Xavier and Marcus. However, Xavier didn't seem to notice since he was too busy dancing and shaking his dreads like Waka Flocka. He was gone off the Molly he had popped earlier before stepping into the club.

2 Chainz "*I Luv Dem Strippers*" was bumping on maximum. Marcus watched as Damonte slowly made his way over towards them with his homeboys in tow.

Here we fucking go, Marcus thought. *I ain't got time for this bullshit tonight.*

Xavier was too busy dancing to notice the few men approaching them, and he damn sure didn't notice that he sloshed some of his beer onto Damonte's t-shirt.

"*Aye man, what the fuck*?!" Damonte yelled in anger.

Xavier finally ceased his wild dancing to survey the minor damage he had unintentionally caused. "My fault, bruh," he apologized.

Marcus politely excused himself from the females, and made his presence known just in case they didn't see him standing right behind Xavier. If any shit were to pop off, he was definitely going to have his boy's back. That's just how he and Xavier rolled. You couldn't have a problem with one without having an issue with the both of them. Their friendship was as strong as two brothers' bonds.

Damonte glared at Marcus, and he and his small posse walked away without uttering another word.

Machine Gun Kelly's "*Est 4 Life*" blared through the speakers of the club, and everyone immediately went ham.

"Fuck they was on?" Xavier asked shaking his head.

"Fuck them lame ass niggas," Marcus said waving off the small altercation. It was obvious that the dude just wanted to try to put a little fear in their hearts, but that wasn't going to happen.

Okay, I see they hide when we come round...

Get the fuck down...

I am from the city from the city where they—BLAOH—love that gun sound!

I am from the city where they ride til the sun down!

"*WATCH OUT*!" a random person screamed.

Suddenly, Marcus noticed Damonte run up with an empty beer bottle in his hand! He was just about to crack Marcus over the head with the Budweiser bottle—Marcus's reflexes instantly kicked in, and he lifted his right arm just in the nick of time!

The glass bottle shattered on Marcus's forearm and painfully sliced his skin open. He barely even noticed the pain as he and Damonte began throwing punches at one another. Damonte's posse quickly jumped in, and suddenly there was a full on brawl in the center of the dance floor.

Xavier jumped in, and fought two guys at once as Marcus tried to hang with Damonte. He fought blow for blow with a bloodied arm and all. Women were screaming and backing away from the altercation, and several onlookers were trying to record the brutal three on two brawl.

"*Worldstar*!" someone called out.

POP!

POP!

High pitched screams accompanied the gunshots and people frantically cleared out. Everyone ran in every which direction, and before Marcus was able to realize what the hell was happening he was roughly shoved to the floor.

The music instantly ceased, and people were screaming, running, and pushing each other to get out the crowded club before they ended up becoming an innocent bystander.

Marcus struggled to stand to his feet. His clothes were bloodied and torn, and for a moment he wondered if he was actually the one who had been shot. He didn't bother to look as he searched through the pack of people running towards the exit.

Suddenly, Marcus noticed Xavier run towards the hallway in the opposite direction. He wiped away the blood trickling from his busted lip, and limped towards the brightly lit hallway after Xavier. The moment Marcus stepped into the narrow hallway that led to the men and women's restrooms he noticed a few droplets of blood that created a small trail. It was obvious Xavier was bleeding badly.

Marcus's stomach churned as he hesitantly followed after his friend. "X!" he called out. "Yo, Xavier?!"

But Xavier didn't bother turning around as he rushed into the men's restroom. With all the screaming and yelling, Marcus doubted that Xavier had even heard him shouting his name.

Marcus quickly made his way inside the men's restroom. Xavier stood in the middle of the floor bending over slightly and holding onto his abdomen. Marcus watched in horror as blood gushed from his wound, and created a small dark red puddle at his feet.

A couple men who had been hiding in the stalls slowly emerged to see what was going on.

Suddenly, Xavier collapsed onto the dirty bloodstained floor. Marcus quickly rushed over to his friend's side.

"*Fuck*!" Marcus screamed. "Somebody get some help! He's been shot!"

He placed his hands over Xavier's trembling hands, and tried his best to slow down the bleeding. Blood seeped from the several deep gashes on Marcus's right forearm, but his own injuries were the last thing on his mind.

Xavier was sweating profusely, and he was losing blood incredibly fast. His eyes opened and closed several times as he felt himself uncontrollably slipping in and out of consciousness.

"You gon' be aight, man. Just hold on," Marcus told him. He then looked at the two men staring down at Xavier dumbfounded. "Man, what the fuck ya'll just standin' there for?!" he barked. "Get some mothafuckin' help! *He's dying*!"

4

Cameron drove past The Shakedown for what felt like the tenth time that evening. She had been tempted to go inside and make it do what it do, but she wondered if she still had it in her. They say 'If you don't use it, you lose it', and Cameron wondered if the phrase was true in her case.

She was just about to park her truck, hop out, and go in the strip club to find out when the sudden nearby resonance of sirens snapped her out of her troublesome thoughts.

"How in the hell did I even end up in downtown Cleveland?" Cameron asked herself.

Forcing herself back to reality, Cameron finally pulled off. One thing was for certain. She needed money. With fall semester classes beginning and the bills that needed to be paid, Cameron needed a source of income and quickly.

After reaching the intersection of 55th and Superior Avenue, she pulled her cellphone out to see if she had any missed calls. There were two missed calls from Marcus over an hour ago.

Marcus, Cameron sighed.

She always thought about him in the back of her mind even when she knew better. However, her love and loyalty would always remain with Jude.

***

The following Monday, Cameron did something she never thought she'd ever have to do. She put in multiple applications at every store that was currently hiring. She didn't discriminate against any position, even if it was a gig flipping burgers.

It was crazy how just months ago, Cameron was yelling she was the baddest bitch up in the strip club, and now she was putting in apps at local fast food restaurants. Talk about a twist of fate. Cameron also hit up every clothing retail store she knew was hiring. After all, fashion was her main interest.

Cameron had promised herself that she was done with the stripping scene after everything she had gone through. The convenient cash would be greatly missed, but she just couldn't deal with all the extra bullshit accompanied with it.

***

Two days and an extensive surgery later, Xavier was finally recovering from the gunshot wound to his stomach. Marcus hadn't left his boy's side since they rushed him to the emergency room aside from when he had to get his own wounds stitched and bandaged.

He had been totally distraught, blaming himself for what had happened. After all, if Marcus had never stuck his dick in Mia's mouth at the male revue, her dude wouldn't have blew down on them at Club Lush.

Marcus barely got an ounce of sleep, and he didn't breathe a sigh of relief until Xavier finally opened his eyes that afternoon.

"What's up man? How you feelin'?" Marcus asked in a concerned tone.

"A lil' sore..."

There was a brief pause before Marcus finally spoke again. "I um...X...man I'm sorry I even got you in this shit," he apologized. "If it wasn't for me takin' that broad in that dressing room at Pandora's Box, her nigga would've never been sweating me," he said. "We would've never got to fightin' and you would've never got shot...If I could take it back I would—"

"Man, you ain't gotta be sorry bruh." Xavier chuckled. "A nigga just happy he ain't out the game. You know what I'm sayin'?"

Marcus chortled and nodded his head. "I feel you...man...I feel you..."

"Who would've thought I would've been the one to get shot just 'cause you decided to get some neck from a broad with a nigga," Xavier joked. He didn't sound the least bit bitter, but Marcus still blamed himself for everything.

He would never feel the same after that shit...

***

A week later, Cameron drove past The Shakedown again. She watched as men filed inside the popular strip club. The Shakedown might have been a hole in the wall strip club, but there was no denying the potential money one could make.

Cameron missed her loyal clientele. She missed the quick cash. Hell, she even missed the rush and excitement of dancing on stage. Cameron had routinely driven past her old place of employment on several occasions. Each time she was tempted to climb back on the pole, but she had made a promise to herself never to return. Besides, she was pregnant—although not showing—and she couldn't disrespect herself or her unborn child by exploiting her body. Even if she did plan on aborting it.

It's not like anyone will even know you're pregnant, a voice in the back of Cameron's mind told her. *And you're not keeping the damn baby anyway. Why not?*

"No. Fuck that," Cameron quickly said. "I ain't getting back on the pole. I'll take any job before I resort to that shit," she told herself.

***

"Good afternoon. Are you looking for anything in particular?" Cameron cheerfully greeted an older Caucasian woman.

"No...just browsing for now," she said nonchalantly.

"Okay. Well let me know if you need assistance," Cameron said.

"Will do."

It was Cameron's second day employed at the Coach store located in Beachwood Place Mall, and she neither liked nor disliked it. For now it was simply a paycheck, and beggars couldn't be choosers in her case.

She had been *this* close to finally giving into her temptation, and climbing back on the pole until she suddenly received a call from the hiring manager at Coach in regards to an open position. Cameron jumped on the opportunity quick, fast and in a hurry. After she got the call she couldn't wait to tell Jude until she suddenly remembered their last conversation.

As much as Cameron hated to admit it, she was wrong and she knew she was wrong. At one point or another she would have to apologize and make up to her man. They were each other's only support systems in this cold, cruel world, and to be honest, she truly was afraid. It wasn't fair to Jude, but Cameron's only defense mechanism was to flee whenever she had an issue.

"You know what? I actually like this wallet," the Caucasian woman spoke up snapping Cameron from her thoughts. "I would like to know how much this costs." She handed Cameron the nude wallet that was stationed on the display case.

Suddenly, from the corner of her eye, Cameron noticed a familiar face enter the store. She watched as Pure Seduction and Red entered the store, and immediately Cameron saw red. It seemed like just yesterday when Pure Seduction and Red had jumped her in the dressing room and broke her hand.

Just seeing the two of them left a bad taste in Cameron's mouth. Pure Seduction probably wasn't even planning on purchasing anything. Knowing her, she probably just walked into the store to get some shit started the minute she saw Cameron, and having her girl, Red beside her gave her all the more ammunition to do so.

Pure Seduction offered a malicious smirk as she tossed her twenty-two inch Malaysian weave over her shoulder for good measure. She looked stunning in a striped Bodycon dress, and a pair of red pointed toe Christian Louboutins. Red looked equally as hot in a pair of $750 Olcay Gulsen pumps and a black Bodycon dress. Her fire engine red hair was pulled into a sleek high top bun.

Cameron was jealous as hell on the low, but she tried her best not to show it. "Let me go and find out right now," she told the woman before taking the wallet to the cash register.

Pure Seduction whispered something in her girl Red's ear, and they immediately went into a hysterical fit of laughter. Cameron rolled her eyes and tried to pay "Dumb and Dumber" no mind.

"$129.95," Cameron said handing the customer the wallet. She made a face and replaced the wallet before leaving the store without as much as a thank you. It was as if she didn't already know that Coach was semi-high end.

"Hypnotic," Pure Seduction sang out. "Long time no see." She offered a phony smile. "I heard my boo Jude got locked up," she said in a fake sympathetic tone.

My boo, Cameron thought. *Oh hell no.* This chick couldn't pass up the opportunity to rub in Cameron's face the fact that she and Jude used to date.

Red smiled devilishly at Cameron loving every minute of seeing Pure Seduction taunt her.

"You must be taking it hard," Pure Seduction said. Her eyes then wandered to Cameron's hair. "And what's up with the new haircut?" she asked. "What? You a dyke now that ya man locked up?" she teased.

She and Red broke into a sadistic fit of laughter, but Cameron didn't see a damn thing funny. If she bit her tongue any harder, the shit would bleed. It was Cameron's second day on the job, and she would be damned if she lost it because she had fed into Pure Seduction's drama and foolishness.

"Oh yeah. And my girl told me she saw you and Marcus leave Club Earth together a couple months ago," Pure Seduction added. She was smiling her ass off by then, and Cameron already expected her to drop a bombshell on her. "I just think it's *so* funny that we seem to have the *exact* same taste in men." She twirled a strand of wavy weave between two fingers. "I mean think about it," she said. "First Silk...then Jude...then Marcus," Pure Seduction giggled. "All I want to know," she began. "Is if you truly enjoy having my leftovers?"

Red burst into a fit of laughter. Cameron was fuming mad inside. She had no idea that Marcus and Pure Seduction had history, but now that she knew, that gave her all the more reason to leave his ass alone.

Cameron's jaw muscle tensed as she fought the urge to grab Pure Seduction by her weave and beat her ass all up and down the Coach store. After all, it wouldn't be the first time she had whupped Pure Seduction's ass for talking and behaving recklessly. One would've thought she would have learned from the first ass kicking, but that obviously wasn't the case.

Swallowing her pride, Cameron forced a smile and said, "If you need help finding anything, let me know."

Red looked at Pure Seduction and they both broke out laughing. "Oh shit, is this bitch serious?" Red asked. She then looked at Cameron with disdain. "Hoe, I could smack that stupid ass smirk off your face," she said.

"Later for that shit," Pure Seduction spoke up. "This bitch ain't even worth it, Red" she scoffed.

"You don't even know what the word *worth* means," Cameron suddenly spoke up. "'Cuz why you're rubbing in my face that you slept with the men I've dated, just know that's all you were. Some easy pussy, while I was the one being splurged on and taken *damn* good care of," she smiled proudly. "Jude and Silk loved me," Cameron noted. "And all you were was just a quick nut."

Pure Seduction's smirk was wiped clean off her face after that remark. She felt so insulted that she barely even had a decent comeback. "Bitch, that's why you're *working* here and I'm *shopping* here," she spat.

Cameron smiled, shook her head, and walked off.

Feeling like she had a point to prove, Pure Seduction began grabbing random Coach bags, satchels, and wallets just because she could. After grabbing several items, she sashayed up to the cash register and placed the items on the counter.

Cameron grimaced as she fought to bite her tongue. Pure Seduction was really trying her. After ringing up and wrapping every item, Cameron bagged up the purses, satchels, and wallets. "Your total is $2486.87," she said flatly.

Red looked confused as to what Pure Seductions motive was.

Pure Seduction handed over her Visa. Cameron knew her ass was up to some shit, but what exactly she had no idea. After swiping the card, the transaction was approved, and Pure Seduction signed the proper receipt before taking her shopping bags and sashaying out of the store.

Cameron watched as Pure Seduction and Red headed towards the exit, and stopped just before they completely stepped out. Pure Seduction leaned over and whispered some sly shit in Red's ear, and Red turned around and smirked at Cameron.

"What are these hoes up to?" Cameron asked herself. It was obvious that the pair was up to no good the moment they stepped inside the Coach store.

Pure Seduction's heels click-clacked as she strutted towards the cash register. "Um...can I see the manager?" she asked Cameron. "I would like to return these items."

Cameron's eyes widened in disbelief. Not only was Pure disrespecting her at her place of business, but now she was fucking up her commission.

"Wait one second," Cameron said dryly before going into the back of the store where the office was located. She could hear Pure and Red giggling like two little ass kids.

Her flamboyant older Caucasian male manager was seated at his desk looking through paperwork when Cameron sauntered in. "There's a customer that wants to see you," she said flatly.

Her manager grimaced, and it was obvious that he didn't feel like being bothered. He switched to the front of the store and put on a fake smile. "Hello ladies, how may I help you today?"

"Hi...um...yes...I would like to return these items and get a full refund if possible," Pure said before placing the shopping bags on top of the counter.

Cameron's manager frowned. "Okay, I'm sorry to hear that, but I will be glad to assist you with that," he said trying to sound as cheerful as possible although he was fuming mad inside. "And why, might I ask, are you returning these items?"

Pure Seduction looked over at Cameron and smiled devilishly. "I was treated very rudely by this employee," she said. "As a matter of fact, she just cost you $2500."

Cameron's mouth fell open. "I treated you rude?!" she repeated in disbelief. "Get the hell out of here. You came in here disrespecting me off rip—"

"Cameron! Cameron!" Her manager cut her off. "Calm down," he told her. "Could you please go wait for me in my office?" His tone was laced with irritation.

Cameron sighed in frustration, and slinked off to the back of the store like a child preparing to be reprimanded by their parent.

Red and Pure Seduction cracked a sneaky smirk pleased with the trouble they had caused. After the manager took care of Pure, they left the store gossiping and laughing at Cameron's misfortune.

The manager of the Coach store immediately made his way to his office. Cameron quickly looked up the minute he stepped inside the room. There was a hopeful look in her eyes, but in her heart she felt desperation. She needed this part time gig. Classes were starting next week and she had maxed out her school loans. She needed the money...badly.

"Cameron, I can't have you disrespecting customers and costing this store sells," he said in a serious tone.

"I didn't disrespect her," Cameron defended herself. "She knows me from...," Cameron paused. "School...and she don't like me. The only reason she even came into the store was to start some mess with me—"

"Look, whatever quarrels you two had with each other should never get in the way of your performance," he said matter-of-factly. "The behavior you displayed out there was totally unacceptable." He sighed deeply. "I'm going to have to let you go, Cameron..."

Tears suddenly formed in Cameron's eyes, but she quickly blinked them away. Her nostrils flared in anger. It felt as if her entire world was crashing down around her. She needed this job. She even considered begging for him to change his mind and give her a second chance, but Cameron had far too much pride to do that.

Standing to her feet, Cameron stormed out of the office and out the Coach store. Once she was in the actual mall, she looked around to see if she saw either Pure Seduction or Red. She planned on beating the shit out of Pure Seduction, and then strangling her afterward.

Cameron, for the life of her, couldn't figure out why Pure's sole mission in life was to make her life hell.

"I swear, I'm gonna kill this bitch!" Cameron seethed.

A few passing people looked at her as if she had just lost her mind, but she didn't give a damn what they want. Cameron was pregnant, broke, alone, and angry. A horrible combination. She vowed that when she got her hands on Pure Seduction she would make her trifling ass feel her wrath.

5

Jerrell walked through the prison rec room towards the table where there were several old heads playing cards. Unfortunately, he and his brother Jude had been placed in two separate correctional facilities, and Jerrell couldn't help but feel like the judge had purposely done that shit out of spite.

He pretty much stayed to himself for the most part, but when and if he felt like being social, he usually interacted with the older inmates. The younger ones were too rowdy and arrogant, and Jerrell didn't have time to be trying to fight anyone and risking more time getting tacked onto his seven year prison sentence.

Jerrell's thoughts were suddenly interrupted when a strong shoulder knocked against his, practically causing him to lose his balance.

"*Oomph*!" he grunted in pain. "Aye, what the fuck is your problem?!" Jerrell yelled in anger.

The guy who had just assaulted him turned around and smirked. Jerrell recognized the nigga immediately. He was one of the guys Jerrell fought back at Buffalo Wild Wings Grille and Bar. Some cat had assaulted Cameron in the restroom hallway. He could remember the afternoon vividly almost as if the shit had happened last night.

After Jude stole on his friend, his homeboys jumped in, and then he and his cousins joined the fight, and it was on and popping.

Darnell mean-mugged Jerrell and waited for him to jump stupid. Jerrell had him as far as weight, but Darnell had the upper-hand in the height department standing at six feet three inches. "Nigga, you my mothafuckin' problem!" Darnell spat.

A few inmates turned their attention in the direction of the two men. They just knew a conflict was about to arise. There wasn't a day that went by that a fight didn't break out. Too much testosterone could do that to a place.

Jerrell clenched his fists tightly and walked up in Darnell's face. "Well then, nigga, do somethin' about it," he said. "Don't talk me to death." His self-promise to avoid drama had completely gone out the window the moment he was disrespected.

Darnell roughly snatched up Jerrell by the collar of his navy jumpsuit. "Nigga, I'll break yo' weak ass—"

"Fuck off me!" Jerrell spat before shoving the hell out of Darnell.

Before Darnell could even retaliate, Jerrell threw a vicious punch that connected with Darnell's jaw. His head snapped back as he uncontrollably stumbled backwards.

EEERRRRGGGGHHHHH!

The prison alarm went off signaling that a domestic dispute was in progress. Every inmate in the rec room dropped down onto the dirty tile floor. Anyone still standing would be thought of as a threat. Correctional officers quickly rushed downstairs preparing to break up the fight.

Darnell and Jerrell tried to rip each other apart, but with several correctional officers holding each man back, their attempts were useless.

"*Mothafucka, you dead*!" Darnell screamed. His cheek had quickly swelled up from the vicious blow. "You hear me, nigga?! *You fuckin' dead*!"

***

Many thoughts ran through Jude's mind as he was escorted to the prison visitation room. His emotions were in shambles, and Cameron was the one to blame. He hadn't spoken to her since their last visit, and he truly didn't know where they stood in one another's life. He loved that girl more than he loved himself, but he would be lying if he said that Cameron didn't hurt him with the painful words she had said. Jude honestly didn't believe she knew just how much he needed her.

Cameron slowly made her way towards Jude's table where he sat with an expressionless look on his face. His dreads were pulled back, and she actually noticed for the first time that he was getting a little stockier. She wasn't surprised though. Cameron knew there really wasn't much to do behind bars *but* work out. The added weight and muscles actually looked good on him.

Jude slowly stood to his feet the moment Cameron reached his table. She gradually made her way towards him. He pulled her into a strong embrace holding on as tight as he could without hurting her in the process.

"I'm sorry baby," Cameron whispered as she buried her head in Jude's firm chest. She wrapped her hands around his waist.

Jude kissed the top of her hair and hugged her tightly. He needed Cameron to know and feel just how much she truly meant to him. "Don't you do that," Jude told her. "Don't you ever do that shit to me again, you hear me?"

Cameron looked up into Jude's earnest eyes and nodded.

He bent down and kissed her passionately, not giving a damn about the CO in the corner of the room clearing his throat sarcastically.

When they finally pulled apart to catch their breaths, they had a seat opposite of each other at the cold metal table.

Cameron decided to speak first, and this time, she wasn't going to start the conversation off about the baby she was carrying. It was already a touchy subject to begin with, and she still had yet to schedule "the appointment."

"I've been looking for a job," she said. "Well...I *had* one," she corrected herself. "I worked two days at the Coach store in Beachwood Mall and ended up getting fired."

Jude looked genuinely disappointed. "How'd that happen, bay?" he asked.

Cameron snorted. *"Hmph.* Two words…Pure…Seduction." Just saying the chick's name left a bad taste in her mouth.

Jude scoffed and rolled his eyes. "Bay, you can't be lettin' these hoes get under your skin," he told her. Bitches just wish they had what you had," he said. "Don't give 'em the satisfaction of knowin' they got to you. Ya dig?"

Cameron nodded her head. "I feel you," she answered. "But now it's a little too late for me to abide by it," she said. "I'm right back at square one. My money's dwindling. Classes start in a matter of days…I need books…bills need to be paid—"

"Sell my car," Jude suddenly said.

Cameron looked surprised to hear him say such a thing. "Excuse me?" She had to be sure she was hearing her man correctly. Did Jude just tell her to sell his precious 2012 Fisker Karma? The prize of his life?

"Sell my car," he repeated. "Sell the furniture in the condo. Do what you gotta do—"

"I can't sell the things you worked hard for," Cameron said shaking her head.

"You need the money," Jude said as if she already didn't know she was broke as a joke.

"I just can't do that, Jude," Cameron argued. "I just can't do that—"

Jude reached over and lightly touched Cameron's hands. "Bay, I'ma need you to push your pride to the back of ya mind for now," he told her. "I don't give a fuck about that car when it comes to you. Straight up," he said. "I'm not 'bout to sit here and watch you struggle if it's somethin' I can do—shit, if it's anything I can do. You feel me? Sell the car," he said with finality. "All the documents are in the glove compartment."

Cameron remained silent as she stared at her man. She couldn't believe that he was sacrificing something so precious just for her. Suddenly, she felt really badly about the things she had said during their last visit. She felt worse for even thinking about giving up on him especially when he had displayed the requited love he had for her time and time again.

There was an uncomfortable silence between them. She really wasn't feeling the idea of selling his car, but he was right. She needed the money.

"So...," Jude began. "About the pregnancy—"

"I don't wanna talk about the pregnancy," Cameron cut him off. She dreaded even thinking about it, but she just knew the topic would arise eventually. She was only a month pregnant, and it seemed to dominate her entire life.

Jude sighed in frustration. "Okay," he agreed. "We don't gotta talk about the pregnancy right now," he said. "But at one point or another, we're going to have to."

Cameron grimaced. "Fair enough..." She cleared her throat and sat up in her seat. "So have you talked to your brother?" she asked, anxious to change the subject. "How's he holding up?"

"He's straight. Just tryin' to stay up. Still salty as hell they ain't put us in the same facility," Jude said. "But enough about my brother...I wanna know what's up with you," he said. "Are you with me, Cameron?" Jude asked.

"Of course I'm with you," Cameron answered. "I'm here aren't I—"

"Nah, you ain't hearin' me," Jude cut her off. "I mean...are you *really* with me? Are you here 'cuz you feel obligated to be...or are you here 'cuz you really wanna hold a nigga down?"

Cameron placed her soft hands over Jude's. "I'm here because I love you," she answered truthfully. "I know the last time we spoke I made you have your doubts about me." She sighed dejectedly. "I was just going through some shit bay...I'm really sorry that I took it out on you. But baby, you don't have to wonder about my loyalty because it's with you...and it'll always be with you."

Jude smiled hearing the sincerity in his woman's voice. He nodded his head in admiration. "You just don't know how good that shit makes me feel hearing you say that." He chuckled. "Yo, I might be on lockdown, but that shit just made me feel like the luckiest nigga alive. Real talk."

***

"What's up, young blood? How'd the visit go?" Jude's roommate Larry asked. He then held his hands up in mock surrender. "My fault, is it aight if I *ask* you how ya visit was?" he said in a sarcastic tone.

Jude took a seat on the stool in front of the desk. "It was straight," he answered nonchalantly.

Larry was confused. "So why do you look like somebody just damn died?" he asked.

Jude shrugged and ran a hand through his dreads. "I hate the fact that my girl strugglin' without me, you know?" he said. "She's in school and shit...tryin' to manage the bills and everything else...I'm just fucked up about the fact that a nigga can't be there for her." Jude then thought about how he had told Cameron not to resort to stripping, and wondered if he was selfish for being that way. But then again, what man would be content with their woman climbing a pole for a living? He sure as hell wasn't.

Larry nodded his head in understanding. "Finances could be a bitch, right?" he asked.

Jude snorted. "A dirty bitch," he added. "I'm in this mothafucka rottin' away, and I can't do shit to help her. I mean it ain't like I can get money in this mothafucka," he said bitterly.

Larry's eyes widened as he looked away. He obviously knew something that Jude didn't.

Jude didn't miss the look. "Come off of it," he said.

Larry ran a hand over his balding hair and sighed deeply. "There's ways..." was all he said.

Jude sat up in his seat, and folded his toned arms across his chest. Written in big, bold cursive on his left forearm was the word 'Loyalty', and on his right forearm was the word 'Respect'. Two things he stood firmly by in life.

"Enlighten me," he said.

Larry sat upright in bed, and glanced at their closed door as if he were expecting a correctional officer to be sneakily looming around. "I can tell you how," he said. "But I gotta admit...I'd hate to see you caught up in some illegal shit. Especially when you only lookin' at five years...Shit, that may as well be a slap on the wrist."

Jude stared intensely at his roommate. "I don't give a fuck what I gotta do when it comes to takin' care of my girl..."

***

I'll beat the pussy up, up, up, up, up, up, up...

I'll beat the pussy up, up, up, up, up, up, up...

Marcus pulled his duffel bag from over his shoulder and dapped up a few fellow dancers as he stepped inside Pandora's Box. LoveRance and 50 Cent's single "*Up*" blared through the massive speakers in the club.

Pandora's Box wasn't as crowded as it was the night of Punisher's birthday bash, but it was still enough women in the club to clean up if you were on your A game, and Marcus always brought his A game. However, he was feeling a little out of sync tonight since his homeboy was still in the hospital. As a matter of fact, he wasn't feeling much like himself at all, but he tried to push the shit to the back of his mind for the sake of making money. After all, a nigga had to eat.

"Hey ladies, how're you doing this evening?" he greeted several women seated at a nearby table.

"Better now that you're here," one responded.

After exchanging a few pleasantries with the customers, Marcus headed to the dressing room. There were several male dancers inside preparing for their upcoming performances. A few were busy getting dressed while one jacked his dick off to an Issue of VIBE magazine with Kelly Rowland covering her bare breasts on the cover.

Everyone had their own means of preparing for their show. Marcus took a seat next to Pleasure who was snorting a line of cocaine off the vanity's countertop. Marcus dropped his duffel bag beside the empty chair, took a seat, and prepared to pull out his pills.

"Aye, nigga, you tryin' to do a line with me?" Pleasure asked before wiping away the residue from beneath his nose.

He offered the drug much like he was offering a cup of coffee or a peppermint. One would never know he was actually a coke head just by looking at him. He resembled actor Omari Hardwick. Ttribal tattoos adorned both his muscular arms from his shoulders down to his elbows.

Marcus's eyes focused on the white powder sitting temptingly on the counter. He had promised himself that he would never fuck with that shit saying that he was perfectly content with popping. However, he was extremely stressed about his homeboy...He needed something a little stronger than an ecstasy pill to ease his mind. Hell, why not?

"Fuck it," Marcus shrugged nonchalantly. "I'll do a line."

6

Jude had told Cameron to sell his car, but she had no intentions of doing that. As a matter of fact, it would be her last resort. With three days left before Fall Semester classes began, Cameron needed a part time gig and fast...something that would pay well.

On a whim, Cameron found herself applying for a position as a bartender at the 216 Lounge located on the east side of Cleveland. She had stumbled across the opening via an ad on Craigslist. Never bartending a day in her life, she had no experience whatsoever but she prayed that fact wouldn't hinder her.

Dressing up for the first time in a long time, Cameron looked mature and sexy in a nude Lanvin cashmere dress, and brown leather over-the-knee boots. There were only a few customers inside the bar during happy hour, but all the men inside made it their mission to eyeball the young, curvaceous woman strutting inside. Mouths watered as they watched her hips and ass sway through the fabric of the cashmere dress.

After speaking briefly to the manager, she was given an application that she wasted no time in filling out in the farthest corner of the lounge. Cameron tried to ignore the penetrating stares of the men eyeing her from the bar. Hell, they were just being men. However, she felt as if someone was staring a lot harder than the rest.

Lifting her gaze briefly from the job application, Cameron slyly looked over at the bar. One face immediately stood out...

Cameron's face flushed in shock and anger as she stared at the pair of dark, cold eyes glaring at her. It felt as if she had just seen a ghost as she watched her worst enemy's thick lips curl into a sadistic smile.

The motherfucker then actually had the nerve to wave at her. He raised his Corona in the air.

"Fat bastard," Cameron mumbled under her breath.

She then refocused her attention back on the application, and tried to pay the son of a bitch no mind. The blue Papermate pen shook in Cameron's trembling fingers as she scribbled in the fields.

So many painful memories invaded her thoughts. Images of her being punched in the face and pinned down to a stiff bed suddenly came to mind. Picturing a scratchy tongue being forced into her mouth while she was brutally raped nearly caused Cameron to vomit.

"Here you go," a female bartender spoke up interrupting Cameron's painful memories. She placed a glass of white wine in front Cameron. "Complements from the gentleman at the bar." She pointed in Wallace's direction. He was smiling his ass off knowing that he'd gotten under Cameron's skin.

Gentleman my ass, Cameron thought. "Thank you," she forced out.

The bartender walked off, and Cameron hurriedly finished her application. She then made her way towards the bar having not touched the drink Wallace had brought her. "I'm all done," Cameron said handing her application to the manager. She could feel Wallace's no good ass watching her every move.

The manager quickly scanned over Cameron's application, asked her a few standard questions, and surprised her when he asked when's the soonest she could start. Of course her response was as soon as possible, and he promised that he would give her a call at his earliest convenience.

Feeling satisfied, Cameron made her out of the bar trying her hardest not to look in Wallace's direction even though everything in her wanted to grab a wine glass, smash it against the bar, and slit his throat with the sharpest shard. He had made her life a living hell, and he only seemed to take pride in the mental damage he had caused.

Cameron's heels click-clacked against the asphalt as she made her way across the street towards her Audi q7 parked alongside the curb. A swift breeze blew, and for the first time she actually missed her hair, and the fact that it kept her head warm.

Pulling out her car keys, she unlocked and opened the driver's door—

THUNK!

A dark hand suddenly appeared out of nowhere, and quickly slammed the car door shut in her face!

Cameron slowly turned around and faced Wallace. He looked surprisingly calm, but irritated nonetheless. He effortlessly pinned her body against her truck with his own.

"So that's how you gon' do a nigga?" Wallace asked with a slight smirk. "I bought ya ass a drink, and you act like you ain't even see the shit," he said.

Cameron forced a smile just to spite him. "I barely saw you," she said through clenched teeth.

"Bullshit," Wallace said in a low tone. "I bet ya clit got to jumpin' the minute you saw me." He suddenly reached down and grabbed Cameron's crotch through the thin fabric of her cashmere dress.

Cameron quickly slapped his hand away feeling violated. "Nigga, don't you ever fucking touch me!" she yelled in anger.

Wallace pressed his body firmly against Cameron's so that she could clearly feel his erection through his True Religion jeans. He found her anger amusing, and it was actually turning him on even more.

"How many times we gon' do this?" Wallace asked with a sly grin. "I mean, shit," he shrugged. "We keep runnin' into each other...must be meant to be, right?"

"Get away from me Wallace..." There was actually a hint of fear in Cameron's shaky tone.

"Or what?" Wallace spat. "Fuck you gon' do to me? Gimme a lap dance?" He chuckled at his own crude humor.

He then peered into her car and then glanced around at their surroundings.

There wasn't another person in sight, and Cameron could only imagine the evil things running through Wallace's fiendish, perverted mind.

"The man ain't around, huh?" Wallace asked referring to Jude. A sneaky smile then formed on his lips.

Suddenly, Cameron raised her hand to slap the shit out of Wallace, but he caught her arm in mid-strike.

Cameron winced in pain as Wallace squeezed firmly on her forearm, threatening to snap her bone in two. "*Aaahh*!" she yelped pain.

"Bitch, you gon' quit playin' and gimme what the fuck I want!" he yelled. Spit splattered onto her face as he shouted.

"You already got what all you gon' get out of me!" Cameron said through gritted teeth. Tears streamed down her cheeks, and she just knew Wallace was on the verge of breaking her arm.

SCREEEEEECCCHHHH!

Suddenly, the tires of a custom gunmetal black Chrysler 300 burned the asphalt as the passing driver brought his car to an immediate stop.

Cameron never thought she'd be so happy to see Marcus. He quickly hopped out the driver's side, leaving his car parked crookedly in the middle of the street.

He walked hastily around his car and towards Cameron and Wallace. “Is it a mothafuckin’ problem?!” he asked looking at Wallace specifically. His fists were clenched tightly, and he was ready to go for a round two with Wallace if need be.

“Nah…none of that,” Wallace answered dumbfounded.

“Then I suggest you get ya damn hands off my girl before I knock ya mothafuckin’ fronts out, nigga!”

Whoa! *My girl,* Cameron thought. A smile involuntarily tugged at her lips. She was so grateful for his presence.

Wallace hesitantly released Cameron’s arm. He didn’t want it with Marcus, especially after he had gotten his shit rocked the last time they bumped heads.

Without another word, he walked towards his car parked a few cars down from Cameron’s, hopped in, and skirted off. He was actually childish enough to flip Cameron and Marcus off as he drove past them.

“Fucking pathetic,” Cameron muttered before wiping her tears away.

Marcus didn’t give a damn about his car still parked in the middle of the street as he walked over towards Cameron. She appeared visibly upset and shaken up.

“You aight?” Marcus asked in a concerned tone.

Cameron nodded her head as she held onto her sore arm.

"What are you doin' here?" he asked her.

"I was just seeing about getting a job here—"

"A job?!" Marcus cut her off. "Cameron, you don't wanna work in this hood ass bar—"

"I have bills to pay," she interrupted him. "And I have to take care of myself. I danced for a year," she reminded him. "I'm sure I can handle any job now..."

Marcus stepped uncomfortably closer to her. "Cameron, you know if you ever need anything, I told you, all you gotta do is gimme the word. I don't even know why you're runnin' and hidin' from me," he said. "I'm not like these other niggas out here. I don't want shit from you. You know that..." Marcus then looked down to see Cameron cradling her arm. He carefully lifted her arm to examine the damage, and frowned at the sight of the reddish-bluish bruise left after Wallace grabbed her. Even his handprints were still clearly visible.

"Dude, next time I see this nigga, I'm breakin' my foot off in his ass," Marcus said. "What is it with you and that dude anyway?" he asked in an irritated tone.

Cameron snatched her arm away from Marcus obviously offended by the question. "Nothing," she said flatly. "Not a damn thing."

Marcus saw her irritation and decided to change the subject. "Cameron, why do you be avoidin' me and ignorin' my calls?" he asked.

"I'm going through some shit," she said.

"Oh yeah...with ya man bein' locked up, right?" he asked.

Cameron stared at Marcus in disbelief. It seemed like the entire city knew about Jude's imprisonment. She didn't know if Marcus had said that to purposely throw up in her face the fact that her man was in jail or if he was being genuine, but either way the comment rubbed her the wrong way.

Without another word, Cameron opened the door of her truck.

"Cameron—bay, I wasn't tryin' to say the shit like that. Damn. Why you so cold to a nigga?" he asked.

Cameron turned around to face Marcus. His arms were outstretched, and he actually looked disappointed.

"I'm not your bay and I'm not your girl," she corrected him. "Get that through your head, aight? That kiss...," she shook her head. "That shit was a mistake and it'll never happen ag—"

Before she could even finish her sentence, Marcus suddenly crushed his lips against hers. She didn't see it coming at all, and as much as she wanted to push him away and slap him for his impulsiveness, she didn't.

His kiss was gentle, but captivating as their lips pressed together and their tongues danced in unison. Marcus wrapped his hands around Cameron's tiny waist and pulled her closer as he nibbled on her bottom lip.

Suddenly, a soft moan involuntarily escaped through Cameron's lips, and she quickly snapped back to reality. Pulling away from Marcus, she quickly hopped into her truck, started the ignition and peeled off. Marcus stood in the street breathing raggedly and feeling confused as ever.

"The hell is this chick *on*?" he asked himself.

7

"If you would like to accept the charges, press one."

Cameron pressed 1 and held the phone to her ear. Seconds later, she heard Jude's deep melodic voice fill the receiver. "Hello? Cameron?"

"Hey, babe. I'm here."

"What's up?" he asked. "You sound tired...or frustrated..." He wasn't sure which one it was.

"Ran into that idiot today while I was putting in applications." Cameron didn't want to come outright and say that she had applied for a bartending position. She wasn't quite sure how Jude would take that.

"What idiot?" Jude asked in a serious tone.

Cameron suddenly felt foolish for even mentioning it to Jude. The last thing she wanted to do was to get him worked up. Especially when there was nothing he could do about it.

"Never mind," she quickly told him.

"Nah, never mind nothin'," Jude said. "What idiot? What happened?"

Cameron sighed into the mouthpiece. "Jude...it's not a big deal. Really," she added.

"Well if it's not a big deal then tell me the shit," he said in irritation. He then sighed in frustration not meaning to sound so pushy. "You can tell me. For real," he said in a more comforting tone.

Cameron blew air into the mouthpiece of the phone, and shifted her weight from one leg to the other. "Wallace...," she said in a low tone. She hated even saying the son of a bitch's name. "I ran into him today..."

"Wallace?!" Jude repeated. "The mothafucka I almost had to kill when he came to our house on that trash?!"

"This is why I didn't want to tell you," she said. "I didn't want you flipping out—"

"Flippin' out?!" Jude repeated in disbelief. "Hell yeah, I'm flippin' out! I'm on lockdown and I can't do shit to protect you!"

"Jude—"

"You need a gun, Cameron." It was more a statement than an actual question.

"Jude, you know I don't know anything about any damn guns."

"Well, you'd better get to learning," he told her. "There's a gun in my fire safe. The combination is—"

"Jude, I don't want a gun—"

"Cameron, would you just listen to me?! Dammit!" he lashed out. "You can be so fuckin' bullheaded sometimes, man! Now look, I ain't gon' be there to protect you if this mothafucka ever step crazy to you again!" he said. "And you gotta be able to protect ya own self. Not just from him, but from any mothafucka," he added. "You hear me?!"

Cameron nodded her head absentmindedly.

"Cameron, I said do you hear me?" Jude repeated.

"Yes...I hear you."

"I hope you do. And I hope you listen," he said. "Man, I don't know what the fuck I'd do if something happened to you or the baby," he said in a calm tone.

Cameron's heart felt like it had dropped to the pit of her stomach. Unbeknownst to Jude, she had scheduled an abortion that was to take place in two days. She needed to go ahead and get it done now, because the further along she got the more costly the procedure could get. The last thing she wanted was to have a baby scraped out of her at five months.

Jude interrupted Cameron's thoughts as he rattled off the combination to his fire safe located on the upper shelf in the walk-in closet.

"Jude, I don't even know how to shoot a damn gun," Cameron said matter-of-factly.

"It's not hard," he told her. "You just cock the Glock and pull the trigger. It's already a full clip in there."

Cameron didn't even know what the hell "cock the Glock" meant, and she didn't want to tell Jude that, and risk him flying off the handle.

"Look, babe, I gotta go," Jude said. "Know that I love you...and take care of my baby," he reminded her before disconnecting the call.

Cameron hung up the phone and lightly touched her flat tummy. "Oh...I'ma take care of the baby, alright," she told herself.

***

Cameron walked past the walk-in closet in her bedroom several times, before finally mustering up enough courage to step inside, and retrieve Jude's fire safe. After inputting his combination code, she slowly opened the safe...

A polished 9mm pistol was positioned on top of a stack of important of documents. Cameron didn't know the first thing about a damn gun. The only protection she had was a four inch automatic switchblade. And even that weapon could be useless during certain circumstances.

Cameron slowly removed the gun and held it in her hands. It was lighter than she imagined. Running her hands over the barrel, she couldn't help but wonder what it would feel like to pull the trigger...

***

Stone Sanchez made over ten thousand dollars a month selling drugs in prison. Two years ago he convinced a correctional officer to purchase him a cell phone where he called trusted contacts who smuggled in his product for him to distribute in the prison. The guard was compensated handsomely just to turn his head in other direction, and allow Stone to do his one two, all the while keeping his mouth closed.

Two years later, Stone was running a lucrative drug operation inside the prison. He had several soldiers inside working for him, but those individuals were only the most trusted and loyal. Needless to say, Stone's eyebrows were raised in skepticism the moment Jude approached him about working for him.

Stone was an intimidating looking man standing at six feet four inches tall and virtually tattooed on damn near every inch of his body. Devil horns were tattooed on his forehead, and he was once a member of the infamous Mexican mafia.

Stone wasn't feeling the idea of letting Jude join him team. After all, Jude was black and he didn't know the kid from Adam. He really wasn't prepared to take a chance on someone who could possibly be the downfall of his empire. However, Stone decided to give Jude an opportunity to prove himself wrong.

***

Cameron was shocked and elated to receive a call from the manager at 216 Lounge the following afternoon telling her to come in that evening to begin her training. It was obvious that he desperately needed employees, and Cameron definitely lucked up on the position.

She still did not plan on telling Jude about the job. After all, what he didn't know wouldn't hurt him. She would simply tell him that she got a job bagging groceries at some restaurant. Cameron honestly didn't want to hear his mouth, because all he would do was disapprove of it, and at that point she desperately needed income.

"Time to make it do what it do," she told herself.

***

Early in the morning...

When she's all alone...

I'ma take my time...

Do it how we want...

Just to set the mood girl I brought some Marvin Gaye and Chardonnay...

Marcus went ahead and decided to answer his cell phone since the caller seemed intent on speaking to him.

"Yo, what's up?" he greeted nonchalantly.

"You," a familiar voice purred into the receiver.

Marcus turned over onto his back in his Oxford leather king size bed. "What's good?" he asked staring at the deep tray ceiling.

"I hear you be running with Cameron now," Pure Seduction said.

"What of it, girl?" he asked in an irritated tone. He knew Pure didn't call him just to get some shit started.

"You know she's no good," Pure said. "She's a whole lot of drama..."

Marcus chuckled. "And you aren't?" he asked.

"I may be," she agreed. "But all my friends haven't mysteriously died."

"You don't know what that girl's been through," Marcus said. "So stop it."

"Can I ask you a question, Marcus?" Pure Seduction began. "How long were you waiting for Silk to get the hell out of the picture for you to make your move?" she taunted. "I mean, shit, nigga, you must've been prayin' for that dude to die, huh?"

Marcus sighed in disappointment. "You done?" he asked.

"I mean seriously Marcus. You and Silk were like best friends, right?" she reminded him. "You don't think anything's wrong with the shit you doing?"

Pure Seduction was finally beginning to get under Marcus's skin. "Me and Silk did a couple shows together, and that was it, aight?" he said. "We were cool, but never no best friends or no shit like that," he corrected her. "And what's all this shit about anyway? Huh, Pure? You mad another chick besides you is on my mind?"

"That bitch'll never be me," Pure said coolly. "I'm tellin' you Marcus, you need to leave that chick alone," she warned him. "You might think you know her...but trust me, you don't know shit about her..."

8

Now she want a photo...

You already know though...

You only live once, that's the motto nigga YOLO...

And we 'bout it every day, every day, every day...

Like we sittin' on the bench, nigga we don't really play...

Drake and Lil' Wayne's "*The Motto*" blared through the speakers of the 216 Lounge. It was fairly crowded on a Saturday evening. People were wall to wall, posted up, sipping, and conversing without a care in the world inside the popular bar. Since Cameron had no experience in bartending, she had to be trained to learn to make the drinks as well as proportioning them, and Kiana aka "Ki Ki" Banks was unfortunately stuck with the unenthusiastic task of having to train her.

The moment Ki Ki laid eyes on Cameron, she immediately didn't like her. In her opinion, Cameron looked bougie and stuck up in her black open slit wrap skirt, and black mesh crop top that revealed an ample amount of cleavage. Ki Ki just knew Cameron was trying to show her up, and the last thing she wanted was for Cameron's ass to tap into her tips for the evening.

Ki Ki was an attractive, thicker woman but her self-esteem had dwindled over the last couple of years due to the verbal abuse from her baby daddy, RJ. With smooth coffee brown skin, and slanted hazel eyes, she was an attractive woman that didn't see or believe in her own beauty, especially after popping out two kids and having gained seventy plus pounds.

Ki Ki was nowhere near as dressed up as Cameron wearing a pair of black jeggings that hugged her massive thighs and round ass, and a black slit sleeve knit top.

"Here, can you hand this to the ladies sitting at the end of the bar," Ki Ki asked in her thick southern accent. She was born and raised in Georgia and relocated to Ohio four years ago.

Cameron took the two Long Islands from Ki Ki and strolled down to the end of the bar. Every man sitting at the bar's eyes were fastened to Cameron's shapely body, and Ki Ki was hating on the low. She was used to the flirtatious stares and attention on her during her shift, but now Cameron was effortlessly soaking it up without even trying.

Cameron made her way towards two brown skinned women chatting and laughing together at the end of the bar. The moment she got close enough to the females she recognized one of their faces. Cameron immediately froze in place.

Although Cameron was only staring at a side profile, she knew without a doubt that she was looking dead at Silk's sister, Tamika. Images of Tamika punching her in the face at Silk's funeral quickly came to mind. She may have been tripping, but she could damn near taste the blood in her mouth. Tamika blamed Cameron for her brother's unexpected suicide...and up until recently Cameron did as well.

"Why do I keep running into everybody I'm trying to avoid?" Cameron asked herself. Pushing her thoughts and worries to the back of her mind, she continued over towards Tamika and her friend.

Both women focused their attention on Cameron once she walked up carrying their beverages. The smile that was previously on Tamika's face was wiped clean off the moment she looked into the eyes of the one person she hated with a passion.

"Hell no," Tamika said in a nasty tone. She frowned at the very sight of Cameron as if she were shit stuck on the bottom of her shoes. "Girl, this the bitch I was tellin' you about that my brother used to fuck with," she told her friend.

Her friend looked Cameron up and down with distaste. Cameron remained silent as she stood behind the bar holding their drinks in her hand with a smug expression plastered to her face.

"She the reason my mothafuckin' brother dead," Tamika spat.

Cameron stared intensely at Tamika. She looked a lot like her brother Silk, and that fact alone both irritated and intimidated Cameron. However, she was sick and tired of Tamika blaming Silk's untimely death on her.

"Look, I didn't put the fucking gun in Silk's hand!" Cameron defended herself. "And I damn sure didn't tell him to pull the trigger!"

Tamika's mouth fell open in shock and disbelief. She couldn't believe the nerve of this bitch standing in front of her talking as if she played no part in Silk's self-destruction. She damn sure didn't appreciate the tone Cameron was using with her.

"*BITCH*!" Tamika screamed before unexpectedly smacking the shit out of Cameron from behind the bar.

The force of the slap was so powerful that it sent Cameron stumbling backwards. The drinks flew out of her hands, and the sound of the glass shattering immediately got everyone's attention.

"*Hoe, I'ma kill you*!" Tamika yelled trying to climb over the bar.

Thankfully Tamika's friend held her back from literally climbing over the bar and whupping Cameron's ass.

The manager quickly came from the back of the bar to see what was going on. A few male customers rushed over to hold Tamika back from releasing her rage. She had lost her only sibling, and understandably she was still coping.

Cameron wiped away the small amount of blood on her bottom lip. Once again Tamika had caught her off guard, but she knew that she shouldn't have even responded period. She had allowed her emotions to get the best of her.

Ki Ki quickly rushed over to Cameron's aid after the fact. "Oh my God! Are you okay?!" she asked. She actually sounded genuinely concerned.

Cameron looked down in embarrassment. "I'm fine—I'm okay," she quickly answered.

"Someone get her ass out of my fuckin' bar!" the manager yelled in irritation.

"Bitch, it ain't over!" Tamika screamed as the doorman escorted her from the bar against her will. "You gon' see me bitch! I ain't gon' never forget what you did to my fuckin' brother! Hoe, you better watch your back!" she threatened.

Cameron watched at Tamika was dragged out of the 216 Lounge with her girlfriend in tow. Shaking her head, Cameron quickly made her way towards the women's restroom. Once inside, she stepped into an empty stall, and plopped down onto the toilet seat. She dropped her head into her hands and silently cried and cursed herself.

Tiffany's voice echoed in her mind: *If it wasn't for bad luck, you wouldn't have any at all, Cameron.*

Seconds later, Ki Ki entered the women's restroom. "Cameron?" she called out. "Cameron, you good?" Just minutes ago, she was hating on Cameron on the low, but Ki Ki had to admit that what had just happened to her was indeed some foul shit. She then walked over towards the preoccupied stall, and rapped softly on the door.

Cameron sniffled, wiped her nose, and tried to pull herself together before she said, "I'm fine."

Ki Ki slowly pushed open the bathroom. "Look, I know ya ass ain't sitting in here crying and shit," she said. "You ain't gon' get fired or no shit like that, if that's what you're thinking."

Cameron quickly wiped her tears away. Ki Ki didn't know shit about her. The last thing she was shedding tears about was getting fired. Life just seemed to be taking such a toll on her. And with both of her best friends out of the picture, and her man on lock down she'd never felt so alone in life.

Cameron quickly stood to her feet. "I'm not crying about this job," she corrected Ki Ki.

"So what you cryin' for?" Ki Ki asked. "And why the hell did that chick smack you?"

"None of your damn business. That's why," Cameron retorted before pushing her way past Ki Ki and exiting the restroom.

***

"Do you think you could give me a ride home?" Ki Ki asked. Last call was over an hour ago, and they were finally preparing to leave for the night.

Cameron pulled on her biker jacket, and retrieved her car keys from the pocket. She grimaced and looked over at Ki Ki standing a few feet away from her with her hands on her hips. Cameron's eyes then scanned over Ki Ki from her attire to her long sleek ponytail, to the expressionless look on her face. She honestly didn't want to be bothered with any chicks after everything she had gone through with Pocahontas and Tiffany.

"What would you do if I wasn't here?" Cameron rolled her eyes. She was normally never that harsh and rude, but she was still feeling some type of way about Tamika slapping the hell out of her earlier.

"Usually my dude will come and pick me up from work," Ki Ki answered matter-of-factly. "But he ain't pickin' up his damn phone..."

Cameron sighed. "Where do you stay?" she asked. She wasn't trying to play taxi driver tonight. Truthfully, she just wanted to go home, take a hot shower, climb into her bed and wallow in her own sorrows.

"I stay off of 79th and Superior," Ki Ki answered. "Not too far from here—"

"I know where it's at," Cameron cut her off. "You ready?"

Ki Ki nodded her head and followed Cameron outside to her vehicle. Her eyebrows rose in surprise as she eyed Cameron's clean Audi q7. *Why is she driving this, but working in this dump,* she asked herself.

"This a nice ride," she said nonchalantly as she climbed into the passenger seat.

"Thanks," Cameron responded flatly.

Ki Ki pulled her seat belt across her chest. "You must gotta good nigga at home," she said in a sly attempt to see if a man had purchased her vehicle.

Cameron rolled her eyes, and turned up the volume to 2 Chainz and Nikki Minaj's single "*Beez in the Trap*". She didn't have time for Ki Ki trying to interrogate her and her life.

Ki Ki snorted. "Stuck up bitch," she mumbled under her breath.

Fifteen minutes later, Cameron pulled alongside the curb of Ki Ki's run down duplex. A tan 1997 Toyota Camry was parked in the driveway, and Cameron had a half a mind to ask Ki Ki if her man was home all along.

"Thanks a lot," Ki Ki said. "I really appreciate the ride."

Cameron remained silent as she waited for Ki Ki to get the hell out of her truck.

Ki Ki barely got out the vehicle all the way, before Cameron rudely skirted off. Ki Ki stuck her middle finger up in hopes of Cameron seeing it in the rear view mirror. "Fuckin' bitch," she muttered. "That's why you got smacked in your shit," she said walking towards her front door.

A stray cat ambled towards her, and she kicked her foot in its direction scaring it off. Ki Ki hated living in the most 'hoodest part of the hood', but money was tight and she had to take what she could get. Her nothing ass baby daddy didn't work and the $674 Social Security check he received every month did little next to nothing to provide for her and her two children.

Ki Ki sighed in frustration, and made her way inside her home. Her eyes widened in disbelief as she watched her four year old daughter and two yea old son playfully chase one other around the messy living room. They were screaming and laughing, and barely even noticed their mother enter the house.

"Hey! Hey! Hey!" Ki Ki yelled. "What the fuck ya'll asses still doing up?!"

Her children quickly ceased playing and stared at their angered mother.

"And why this mothafuckin' house look like this?!" she hollered.

Tiana shrugged, and Ki Ki was two seconds away from slapping her harder than Cameron had gotten slapped earlier.

"Where's ya'll daddy at?" she asked with much attitude. RJ was biologicallyonly RJ Jr.'s father, but after being with him for nearly three years Tiana looked at him as her own dad.

"Upstairs," Tiana answered picking the throw pillows up from the dirty carpet and replacing them on the tacky brown sofa.

Tiana was fair-skinned and had inherited Ki Ki's slanted eyes, but most of her Caucasian father's looks. She was a cute little girl with sandy brown curly hair and one dimple in her cheek. RJ looked like a spitting image of his father, and because of that Ki Ki secretly resented him.

"I'm givin' ya'll mothafuckas three minutes to clean my damn house or else I'm beatin' the fuck outta ya'll," she threatened.

Tiana and RJ Jr. quickly proceeded to straighten up the living room. They were just babies, but even they knew how crazy their mother could be especially when upset. RJ still had a small knot on his forehead from when he had peed in the bed last week.

Ki Ki quickly made her way upstairs towards her bedroom. She was infuriated that her man didn't even answer her calls or text messages in regards to picking her up. He was so damn useless to her, but she just couldn't let his sorry ass go. She loved RJ with every fiber of her being, but strangely she hated him just the same. It was a love that even she barely understood.

"Nothin' ass nigga," Ki Ki mumbled under her breath as she stumped up the stairs.

As she neared her bedroom, she heard the unmistakable sounds of a bed creaking. Her heart felt as if it had dropped into the pit of her stomach.

Is that what the hell I think it is, she asked herself. With each step she took towards her closed bedroom door, her heart thumped louder and harder in her chest.

Once she reached her door, she placed her ear against it, and listened to the soft muffled moans coming from the opposite side of the door.

Ki Ki was fuming mad. The nerve of this dirty ass nigga to bring some female into her home!

Without warning, she swung open the bedroom door in a fit of rage! "Nigga, you fucking—" Ki Ki's eyes bulged in their sockets at the unnerving sight before her.

9

Ki Ki felt as if she was trapped in a nightmare. She couldn't believe the shit she was seeing. Her man...in their bed...with another man!

"*Aaaaaaaaahhhhhh*!" A bloodcurdling scream reverberated off the bedroom walls. It took Ki Ki a minute to realize that she was the one who had emitted the scream.

RJ's boy toy jumped out the bed ass naked, his flaccid penis dangling in front of him. There was an uncomfortable period of silence after Ki Ki's earsplitting scream. She looked from her man to the stranger standing in her bedroom and suddenly flipped the hell out!

"*Oh, hell no*!" she yelled charging towards the men.

RJ quickly grabbed, and restrained Ki Ki before she could inflict any damage.

"Get ya fucking hands off me you dirty ass nigga!" Ki Ki thrashed about in his strong embrace.

RJ's lover quickly slipped into his sweatpants and scrambled up his clothes and shoes in hastiness. "Nigga, you told me you were single," he said with much attitude.

"Just get the fuck outta here!" RJ spat clearly embarrassed.

"You nasty mothafucka!" Ki Ki screamed at the stranger. She was trying her hardest to get at him, not giving a damn that he was six feet one and incredibly fit, and that she couldn't even fight. "*I'm gonna fucking kill you RJ*!"

RJ's lover quickly exited the bedroom, and RJ didn't release Ki Ki until he finally heard the sound of the front door slamming shut.

Ki Ki whirled around and spat in RJ's face. "You nasty son of a bitch!" she screamed.

RJ surprised her when he suddenly slapped her in the face. "Bitch, you done lost yo' mothafuckin' mind spittin' on me!" he yelled before wiping the saliva off his face.

Ki Ki was no stranger to his physical abuse, and most of the time she enjoyed it as crazy as it sounded. She grabbed her stinging cheek, and her eyes slowly wandered down towards RJ's bare dick. "*You didn't even wear a condom you sick fuck*?!" she screamed slapping him in the chest. "How long were you doin' this shit?! When did you get this way?!" Ki Ki demanded to know. "When you were in jail?! Were you always fucking dudes behind my back?"

RJ pushed past Ki Ki and made his way towards the hallway bathroom. His silence and nonchalant demeanor was driving Ki Ki crazy. She just had to know the truth.

"And you brought that faggot up in my mothafuckin' house?!" Ki Ki screamed following him into the small bathroom. "Around my fuckin' kids! RJ, you dirty as fuck! Couldn't even pick me up from work 'cuz you too busy blowin' some niggas back out!" she yelled. "How could you do this shit to me?! Am I not enough for you—"

RJ whirled around in fury as he faced his woman. "The fuck you want me to say?!" he yelled. "Bitch, look at yaself! You done got all fat and fucking sloppy! Is that what the fuck you wanna hear?! Huh?!" he asked. "Or do you wanna hear that I'd rather fuck a nigga than jump up and down in that dry ass pussy of yours?!"

Ki Ki's mouth fell open in shock and disbelief. His words stung like fire searing her skin. Without another word, she turned on her heel and raced downstairs past her children who looked frightened due to all the screaming and arguing.

When Ki Ki quickly made her way back upstairs, RJ was busy washing the odor off his dick in the bathroom sink. A look of irritation and frustration was etched on his handsome dark face. He was so engrossed in the task at hand that he didn't even notice Ki Ki raise the ten inch butcher knife above his head before swiftly bringing it down on him.

"*Aaaarrrggghh*!" he cried out in pain.

His flesh tore open as Ki Ki jammed the blade into his upper back! Before he was even able to comprehend that he had just been stabbed, Ki Ki jammed the knife into every part of RJ's body that she could reach.

Screaming out in agony, he backed away from Ki Ki and towards the bathtub. Blood spurted from his mouth, and it felt as if his entire body was on fire as she continued to stab his flesh with the ten inch blade.

"Please Ki! I'm sorry!" he cried out holding his hands up to shield his face.

Ki Ki had completely snapped! "You dirty mothafucka! I hate you! I hate you! *I hate you*!"

Ki Ki ignored his pathetic pleas for her to let up. After all, he didn't let up on his verbal abuse. She viciously stabbed him in the right hand! The sharp blade completely impaled his hand. Screaming in pain, RJ stumbled backwards and tripped on the edge of the tub before falling inside. His head smacked against the shower wall, and his neck snapped killing him instantly.

Ki Ki silently stood over RJ's motionless, naked body as he lay awkwardly in the bathtub. Blood ran from his stab wounds into the porcelain tub and down the drain. His eyes were open and glazed over, staring at nothing in particular.

Not feeling very satisfied, Ki Ki dropped onto her knees in front of the tub and proceeded to viciously stab RJ's lifeless body. Blood splattered onto her beautiful face as she wildly stabbed the knife into his torso over and over again.

For several seconds, Ki Ki repeated the same motion until she finally exhausted herself. Truthfully, she was already a little crazy, but tonight Ki Ki had literally snapped. Standing to her feet, she tossed the knife onto RJ's bloodied body.

Suddenly, the sound of movement behind her caused her to turn on her heel. Her daughter Tiana stood in the doorway with a frightened expression on her face.

***

I wish that I could have this moment for life...

'Cause in this moment I just feel so alive...

Cameron reached over onto her nightstand and retrieved her cellphone. After scanning the caller ID, she pressed the TALK button.

"Hello...," she answered in a muffled voice.

"I'm sorry bay. Did I wake you?" Marcus asked in a concerned tone.

Cameron rolled over onto her side. "I actually was sleep," she admitted.

"My fault," Macus apologized. "Just had you on my mind...wanted to hear your voice..."

Cameron's lips betrayed her as she suddenly found herself smirking. "Well, you hear it," she retorted. "Now I'm going back to sl—"

"Cameron, whatever you're going through right now you ain't gotta push me away to deal with it yourself," Marcus told her. "Like I told you before, I'm here for you, and I care about you. So don't be feelin' like you ain't got no one in ya corner, 'cause you got this nigga right here," he said.

"I'll keep that in mind," Cameron said disimpassioned.

"Let me take you to lunch next week," Marcus suddenly said. "No strings attached," he added. "Real talk, I just wanna see you again..."

Cameron ran a hand through her short hair and sighed. "I'll think about it," she told him.

"That's a good enough answer for me," he said. "You gon' head and get some sleep, bay."

"Good night," Cameron whispered.

"Night," Marcus said.

After disconnecting the call, he opened the French doors that led from his room into his patio. He re-entered his bedroom.

Keisha Thompson aka Pure Seduction slept soundlessly in his bed with the sheets partially covering her nude body. Marcus had dicked her down hours ago and worn her ass out. He cherished the peacefulness, because although he liked Pure, her mouth could get so annoying at times. He couldn't deny that her head game was mean though.

Walking inside his master bathroom, he closed the door behind himself. He was grateful that Pure Seduction was sound asleep so that she wouldn't hear the sound of him snorting a small amount of cocaine up his narrow nostrils.

After Pleasure had given him his first taste of the addictive drug, Marcus had immediately gotten hooked, and there was no turning back now.

***

THUNK!

Ki Ki slammed the trunk of her car closed and made her way to the driver's side before climbing in. The vehicle was already running and she patiently waited for it to cool up. She wasn't too worried about any of her neighbors seeing her drag out the large, black trash bag because people in that particular neighborhood knew better than to be out past a certain hour.

Ki Ki turned up the volume to the radio that was currently stationed on 93.1 WZAK. The soft melodic vocals of "Simply Red" poured through her speakers as she listened to the oldie classic "*Holding Back the Years.*" The song seemed to fit the occasion perfectly.

Pulling out a single Newport, she lit the end, and took an aggressive pull. As crazy as it sounded she felt completely refreshed after killing RJ's trifling ass. Ki Ki was no stranger when it came to taking lives. As a matter of fact, she had killed Tiana's father back in Georgia when she caught him cheating on her. After the chick fled from her home like the little bitch she was, Ki Ki ran into her closet and fetched her 9mm. A bullet to the chest and cheek was the ultimate price Tiana's father had to pay for breaking Ki Ki's heart.

Ki Ki blew out a gust of smoke through her slightly parted lips before switching the gears into reverse. Slowly backing out of her driveway, she prepared to dispose of the large, black trash bag in her trunk.

***

Ki Ki grunted in exhaustion as she lugged the heavy trash bag deep into the woods located off Turney Rd. Her car was parked alongside the road, the hazard lights flashed just in case a vehicle came down the long street.

"It ain't even have to come to this shit RJ," she mumbled under her breath.

A family of nearby deer stood off in the distance frozen in place as they watched Ki Ki. After leaving the trash bag near a mass of shrubbery, she pulled out another Newport and lit it. "I'll let the deer have ya ass," she said taking a pull on the cigarette. Wiping the sweat off her brow, she slowly looked up at the dark sky and full moon. "Love is a motherfucker," she mumbled.

***

Ki Ki stared into her children's bedroom as they slept peacefully. There was a faraway look in her eyes as many thoughts raced through her mind. Tiana and RJ Jr. were far too young to know anything about love and the painful effects it could have.

Subconsciously Ki Ki worried if Tiana would tell anyone what she had seen her do...

***

The following morning, Cameron sat in the driver seat of her truck as she stared off into space. So many thoughts ran across her mind.

How will Jude feel once I tell him I aborted the baby?

How long should I wait before I tell him?

Will I lose him?

With all the questions running through Cameron's mind, she could barely think straight, but one thing she knew for certain was that she couldn't keep the baby. She just couldn't. She wasn't ready to be a parent...especially if she had to do it alone.

After all, Cameron barely got a chance to experience what having a mother felt like. How in the hell was she going to be able to a mother to someone else? Her own had died when she was so young that she barely could remember her. Bounced around from foster home to foster home growing up, she was unable to establish a familial bond with anyone.

With Cameron's first pregnancy, she was nervous and afraid, but at least she had Jude in her corner and she knew he would be there for her...now that he was in prison, she was unsure if she was able to handle the task alone. Truthfully, she knew she was thinking selfishly. Instead of thinking about the life inside of her, she instead plotted on destroying it simply because she was afraid.

Jude's words kept replaying over in Cameron's mind: "*God gave us this blessing a second time for a reason.*"

My mind is already made up, she thought to herself as she opened the driver's door and climbed out her truck.

Beads of perspiration quickly formed on her forehead as she gradually made her way towards the Planned Parenthood Clinic. Her legs felt like spaghetti as she slowly made her way across the parking lot.

Cameron felt as if she were walking the green mile. With each step she took, the reality of what she was about to do was settling in. But in all actuality, she wasn't ready to be a mother. She just wasn't...

10

Stone Sanchez ran a lucrative drug operation inside the prison walls of the Cuyahoga Department Correctional Facility. Trusted contacts smuggled in his sought after product and Stone had several soldiers who distributed it in the prison. A few of the COs knew what was going on, but refused to act on it considering they themselves were loyal customers in Stone's money-making operation.

Jude had sworn off ever getting himself involved in the drug business again. It was just too risky and dangerous for him, and it was because of that he found a more unique and different hustle. However, the very hustle that he played off as legit had landed him right behind bars, now Jude had to disregard his old way of thinking.

I'm doing this shit for my girl and my kid, he constantly told himself. To him, they were well worth the risk of possibly facing more time. Jude just couldn't sit back and watch his girl struggle while he sat on lockdown and did nothing to help. He felt—no he was obligated to be there for her...and for his child. That was just the type of man he was.

"You wanted to see me," Jude said slowly stepping into Stone's cell.

Stone was lifting weights using a laundry sack filled with several hardback books. In prison, you had no choice but to get creative especially as far as exercising. The muscles in his arms flexed as he lifted the heavy sack several more times before placing it at his feet.

Stone then turned to face Jude. He was an intimidating looking man, but as long as trouble wasn't brought to him then no one had to worry about any trouble from him. Nearly every inch of his skin was covered with artwork. His most profound tattoos being the large Chinese dragon tattoo on his back and the devil horns tattooed on his forehead. His shoulder length hair was always pulled back into a slick ponytail.

"How you holdin' up in this zoo?" Stone asked Jude. His voice was a combination of calm, deep, and raspy.

Jude was surprised by Stone's casual question, and he actually released a sigh of relief on the low. The last thing he wanted or needed was to have problems with that man. Not that he was chump or anything of the like...he just knew it would be a lost cause trying to overpower such a powerful man.

"Every day is an uphill battle, but I just take it one day at a time," Jude told him. "Could be worse..."

Stone chuckled. "You damn right it could be worse," he agreed. "Hell, you could be stuck in this cell where the cocksucker above me likes to throw his fecal matter into the ventilation."

Jude frowned. "True..."

"So anyway," Stone began. "I called you here 'cuz you're new to the team...I wanna know who I'm dealin' with...I need to make sure you're sane," he joked.

"I can dig it," Jude agreed.

"So you gotta wife?" he asked. "Kids?"

Jude sighed. "I gotta girl...and a baby on the way."

Stone whistled dramatically and shook his head. He then walked over towards his sink where a pack of Marlboro cigarettes sat. "You want one?" he offered pulling out a single cigarette.

"Nah, I'm straight."

Stone shrugged, lit a match and took a slow pull on the cigarette. "Trust me...you'll be needin' one eventually."

Jude allowed Stone's words to sink in. "On that note, shit, I'll take one," he said.

Stone handed Jude a cigarette and lit it for him. Jude wasn't the cigarette type, and he actually stuck to his good ole Black N Milds, but beggars couldn't be choosers in this case. Puffing on the cigarette, he realized just how bad he really needed that smoke.

Stone walked over to the stainless steel stool and took a seat. "You remind me of my son," he suddenly admitted. "I think that's the only real reason, I even let you in on my operation."

"Word?" Jude asked before releasing smoke through his lips.

Stone chuckled with a distant look in his eyes. "Yeah, you even kinda look like him." He motioned towards his hair. "Minus the dreads of course."

Jude suddenly broke out laughing.

"What's so funny?" Stone asked amused.

Jude pulled himself together. It seemed like ages since he had experienced a good laugh. "Nah, man...it's just...you and kids...don't seem like something that goes together," he said.

Stone guffawed, and it actually looked awkward seeing a man as intimidating looking as him laughing. "What, man? I can't have a kid?" he asked sarcastically.

"Where's your son at now?" Jude asked.

Stone paused. The humor in his expression quickly departed and he took on a serious look. "Dead..."

Jude took another pull on the cigarette and suddenly regretted asking. "Sorry to hear that shit, man."

There was a brief moment of silence between the two men before Stone spoke again. "He was a good kid too, man," he sighed in disappointment. "Dirty ass fucking cop killed him trying to get me," Stone explained. "That's the reason I'm in this motherfucker now...killed the son of a bitch with my bare hands." He held up his hands which were riddled with thick veins. "And then after I killed him, I just kept beating his bloody corpse with my fists over and over." He jabbed at the air in front of him. "By the time I got done with that dirty son of a bitch, he was barely recognizable," Stone explained. "Needless to say, I made sure that motherfucker had a closed casket."

Jude felt unnerved by the story he had just heard, but he could totally sympathize with a father's anger from losing his son.

"These cocksuckers slapped the cuffs on me, and tossed me into this cage promising me I'd never again see the light of day." Stone shrugged casually. "As you can see that didn't really stop my flow at all...Hell, I still got people on the outs that gotta eat, you know? Still gotta family that I got to feed." He nodded his head. "We're on the same shit, you know?"

"Real shit," Jude agreed.

"Well...that's all I gotta say," Stone said. "You can go ahead and get back to your rec time before the boys lock us up in our cages."

Jude nodded. "Thanks for the cigarette," he said before turning to leave. He then stopped at the door and slowly turned around. "Did you really bring me in here today to see who you were dealin' with?" he asked. "Or did you want me to know who I was dealin' with?"

Stone chuckled and nodded his head in admiration. Jude may have been young, but he had the cleverness and perception of a wise old man. "Both," he answered.

Jude allowed his simple word to sink in before he made his way out of Stone's cell—nearly colliding into a man lurking outside of the door. Jude recognized him immediately. He didn't know him personally, but everyone in the tier referred to him as White. He was Stone's loyal right hand man.

White stood at six feet five inches tall, and looked every bit of crazy as he actually was. He had pale skin—hence the nickname he was given—and sunken in eyes and cheeks. A long scar ran vertically down the side of his face and Route 666 was tattooed in bold lettering across his chest.

"The fuck you lookin' at?" he spat. He figured Jude was staring a little harder than he needed to.

Jude opened his mouth to say some smart shit, but quickly decided against it. White had been mean-mugging Jude, and tossing him vicious stares ever since he became a part of Stone's operation, and it was obvious that he wasn't particularly fond of him. For what reason exactly, Jude had no idea, and quite frankly he didn't give a fuck. The only reason he decided not to check that hillbilly looking motherfucker was out of respect for Stone.

Shaking his head, Jude walked off in the opposite direction. He had a feeling that White was eventually going to be a big problem.

***

Tiana and RJ Jr. sat at the rickety wooden dining room table. RJ sat on top of a couple of throw pillows in order to prop him up. He was making an utter mess eating a bowl of Raviolis without a care in the world, and completely oblivious to the fact that his own mother had brutally murdered his father last night.

Suddenly, Ki Ki emerged from the kitchen carrying a sharp edged knife. Her beautiful face was expressionless, and just from looking at her one would never be able to guess what exactly was going through her mind.

"Mommy, where's daddy?" Tiana suddenly asked. "Is he okay?"

Ki Ki slowly made her way over towards her four year old daughter. The knife in her hand hung loosely by her side.

Standing behind Tiana's chair she stared down at her child in silence. She then slowly brought the knife down towards her daughter before mumbling, "Daddy is just fine..."

11

"Daddy just went away to go to work. That's all," Ki Ki lied. She then reached over Tiana, and cut a small slice of lemon half-pound cake before placing it on the plate in front of her daughter.

"Now eat your damn cake and don't ask me no more damn questions," Ki Ki said in a nasty tone.

***

Marcus sat in the visitor's chair beside Xavier's hospital bed. He had made it a priority to visit his homeboy whenever he had a little free time to spare.

"You ain't obligated to sit in here with a nigga. You know that right," Xavier said peeling his gaze away from the television to look at Marcus. "Gotta nigga feelin' like he a charity case or some shit," he joked.

"Come on now," Marcus said. "You know it ain't shit like that man. Hell, if the shoe was on the other foot, I'd want you to show me love, ya dig?"

Xavier nodded his head in understanding and then focused his attention back on the re-run of *My Wife and Kids*. There was a brief period of silence between the two friends before he spoke again. "You know that shit that people be sayin' about seein' their lives flash before they eyes before they know they're about to die?" He continued to stare at the television. "I ain't ever known how true that shit was 'til I experienced it myself."

Marcus remained silent as he listened intently.

"I just knew a nigga was about to be out for the count when I saw all my damn blood," Xavier admitted. "I was like 'damn...this shit is it. This a mothafuckin' wrap for my ass.'" He said. "Now that God gave me a second chance, I feel like I gotta start keepin' it a hunnid with myself and other mothafuckas, you know?" He paused. "Man, I gotta be real with you dawg...I smashed ya girl Pure Seduction twice," he confessed.

Marcus was a little disappointed to hear that, but it wasn't like Pure Seduction was exclusively his either.

"I also looked at Cameron's ass a couple times when she came to the show—"

"Hey! Hey! Hey, bruh," Marcus cut Xavier off. "Now if you touch my Cam, I may fuck around and have to shoot ya ass over her." His tone was laced with humor. "And ya ass won't be so lucky then." Marcus was laughing, but inside he was dead ass serious.

***

The moment Cameron stepped through the doors of the student center it felt much like a welcome relief. It felt like years had elapsed since she had last stepped foot inside of Cleveland State University when in all actuality it was only months.

Cameron missed school. She missed attending classes. She missed raising her hand to ask a question. She missed taking notes. She missed having to do difficult assignments. Hell, she just missed feeling normal. Point blank period.

College felt like a magical door that led to a magical world in which she didn't have to worry about her past, her pains, and the drama that had quickly consumed her life. The only thing different now was that she wouldn't have her girl Tiffany by her side as a major support system. It was because of Tiffany that Cameron even made it through the first three years.

While Cameron was busy napping during classes because she was exhausted from dancing at The Shakedown all night, Tiffany was taking notes for her so that she wouldn't fail. She had Cameron's best interest at heart...well...she used to have Cameron's best interest at heart. An unfortunate turn of events had caused Tiffany to go down a path of self-destruction that ultimately led to her death.

Cameron hated even thinking about the death of her best friend so she quickly shook the thoughts from her head, and tried to push any negative memories to the back of her mind. Today was the beginning of a new semester, and a new page in Cameron's life. It was her chance to prove to herself that she could and would be more than just some orphaned girl turned exotic dancer.

As Cameron made her way towards her first class, she noticed the few stares from her fellow female students. Some were whispering, and looking in her direction while others were shaking their heads in disgust. They were all aware of her old profession as a stripper, and they were judging her without even knowing her full story.

I don't give a damn, Cameron thought to herself. *These bitches don't know me or my life.*

Suddenly, a hand reached out and gently grabbed her forearm. "Excuse me miss lady," a deep voice spoke up.

Cameron quickly stopped in her tracks and stared down at the chestnut colored hand softly holding onto her forearm. Her gaze then wandered up to the stranger who had grabbed her. He was an attractive guy who could have been no older than twenty-three or twenty four years old. He had a low haircut, big bright eyes, and full lips that were surrounded by a neatly trimmed goatee. He instantly reminded Cameron of the rapper Big Sean minus the petite frame and height.

"Can I help you?" Cameron asked pulling her arm away from him. She was used to the guys in school hitting on her. They absolutely adored her while on the other end most of the females hated off in the distance.

"How you doing? My name is Mike," he introduced himself sticking his hand out for good measure.

Cameron hesitantly shook his hand with a puzzled expression on her pretty face. "Do, I know you?" she asked.

Mike chuckled revealing a cute set of dimples. "Nah," he answered. "My homeboy told me about you though," he said.

Cameron didn't really like the sound of that. Scrunching her face up in confusion, she said, "Your homeboy told you about me? What does that mean?"

None of the male students attending CSU knew her intimately because the only men she had ever seriously dated were Silk—which lasted damn near two years—and Jude.

"Nah, it ain't nothing' like that, ma," Mike quickly corrected himself. "He told me that you dance at the strip club over there on St. Clair. Check it, I'm havin' a lil' private party. A few of my niggas, and I would love to have a couple dancers there for entertainment," he explained. "I would love for you to be there and bring one of ya girls if possible."

Cameron looked Mike up and down with disdain. She was upset and offended that he would be bold enough to approach her in school of all places with such an offer. "I don't dance anymore," Cameron admitted in a flat tone.

"Look, I'll pay you and ya girl $500 a piece just to show up at the door," Mike said. "It'll be plenty of fellas there so you and ya girl will definitely clean up on the tip side. And trust me, I don't fuck with any niggas that don't get money," he added confidently.

Cameron wasn't buying that shit. She figured he probably had just gotten his school refund check, and was just looking to front like was balling. She knew how the game went.

"What part of I don't dance anymore don't you understand?" Cameron asked in a low tone.

"Well, look, if you change your mind, hit me up," Mike said before hastily scribbling his cellphone number on a piece of notebook paper. He then snatched the paper out of his notebook and handed it to Cameron. "The party is this weekend," he added.

Cameron reluctantly took the piece of paper from him and watched as he walked off. "The nerve of some of these cocky ass niggas," she told herself shaking her head.

Cameron quickly made her way to her business communications class, but stopped in mid-stride when an unsettling thought came to mind. Walking over to the nearby computer center kiosk, she took a seat and typed in her login information on the CSU homepage website. Cameron quickly scanned her balance due which was well over two thousand dollars. She would need to pay that balance off, and as soon as possible.

As much as Cameron hated the idea of dancing again, that avenue seemed like the only and best way to get the convenient cash she needed. Suddenly Mike's offer didn't seem so bad…

***

Cameron headed straight to work after school without any breaks in between. If her work schedule remained the same that would only leave her a few hours after work to get school assignments done. Cameron didn't like the idea of having to do homework or research while she was tired, but she simply had to do what she had to if she wanted to make it.

The 216 Lounge was understandably slower on a Monday night with just a few regulars here and there drowning their sorrows with booze while watching Sports Center on the large overhead television screens.

Ki Ki seemed pretty distant from Cameron during their shift together. It was obvious that she didn't like Cameron, and Cameron really couldn't blame her. Never was she usually that coldhearted and cynical towards people especially for no damn reason, but lately Cameron hadn't been feeling much like herself. Who would if they had been through all the shit she had gone through?

What the hell am I going to do about the offer Mike proposed to me earlier, Cameron asked herself several times that evening. Five hundred dollars upfront sounded like a pretty good deal, especially considering that she wasn't paid a damn thing to walk through the doors of a strip club. Hell, you weren't even guaranteed tips, and then you still had to tip out. Mike was offering her five hundred dollars just to show up plus whatever she earned in tips. Cameron and whatever girl she decided to bring along with her would be the only dancers there so competition would be nonexistent.

Now the only question is...who am I going to bring with me to the party, Cameron wondered. She hadn't talked to Juicy since she worked at The Shakedown, and they weren't cool all like that anyway. Especially not after she and Pocahontas had left her in Columbus to be raped at the hands of Wallace.

Suddenly, from the corner of her eye, Cameron watched as Ki Ki bent over and retrieved a bottle of Corona from the lowest shelf in the cooler. Cameron's eyes suddenly wandered over her thick and curvaceous body figure.

"Well, I'll be damned," Cameron mumbled under her breath. This was her first time looking at Ki Ki, and really looking at her. She was by no accounts into females, but an idea quickly came to mind. Cameron patiently waited for Ki Ki to finish servicing one of the customers before she finally made her way over towards her. "Hey, Ki Ki. Can I talk to you for a sec?"

Ki Ki tucked her hair behind her ear, and raised her eyebrows in skepticism. "It depends," she answered. "What do you have to talk to me about?"

Cameron didn't miss a beat. "Money," she responded with a serious expression.

All of Ki Ki's prior feelings about Cameron quickly dissipated as her full lips pulled into a smirk. She was interested before Cameron even gave up the details.

Taking her smile as an invitation to continue, Cameron went ahead and explained the details of the private party Mike wanted her to do.

"I've never danced before," Ki Ki admitted. "I mean I don't even think I have the body for that shit," she admitted.

"You've got ass and titties," Cameron told her. "Hell, that's all you need to have."

Ki Ki's self-esteem had been beaten down so badly by RJ that she couldn't even see her own attractiveness. "So you *do* think I have the body for it?" she asked Cameron.

Cameron casually laughed. "Of course," she told her. "Your body reminds me of Buffy the Body. Have you ever heard of her?"

A confused look was etched on Ki Ki's face. "No," she answered. "I haven't," she paused. "So um...you don't think I'm fat?"

"What?!" Cameron asked confused. "No! The hell?" she laughed. "You're straight. You're good!"

Ki Ki had an ear to ear grin on her face after hearing that. Unbeknownst to Cameron, she had secretly created a monster just then.

"So look, he said it's this weekend," Cameron explained. "I'm off...how about you?"

"I'm off too," Ki Ki lied. Actually, she was planning on calling off. This bartender job was not about to hold her back from making some real money.

"Well, do you got any kids? Will you be able to get a babysitter?" Cameron asked.

"No—I don't have any kids," Ki Ki eagerly said. "I'm free. Let's get this money," she smiled.

Cameron nodded her head. "Cool. That's what I like to hear."

Ki Ki took a sip from the shot of Hennessey she had poured herself. "You know what Cameron," she began. "We may have gotten off to a bad start, but I think when it's all said and done...we're going to be the best of friends..."

12

"Ma...," Ki Ki paused. "I need to send the kids to you...permanently," she added. Ki Ki sat on top of her closed toilet seat in her bathroom in the dark. She didn't want to turn the lights on out of fear that she'd see RJ's bloodied lifeless body lying in the bathtub.

Ki Ki's sixty-four year old mother, Abigail sighed into the mouthpiece of her telephone. "Ki Ki now you know I am too darn old to be taking care of some babies," she explained in a tired tone. Ki Ki had just wakened her from a peaceful slumber in the middle of the night. "And what's so important that you can't take care of your own children?" Abigail wanted to know.

"For real ma," Ki Ki said in a serious tone. "I think...I think I'ma hurt 'em," she admitted.

Abigail sighed in frustration. "Oh Lord, Kiana," she said. "Have you been taking your medication?" she asked. Abigail blamed herself for her daughter's mental illness, chastising herself for even having a child at the age of forty.

"Ma, I hate when you fuckin' say that word to me," Ki Ki said. "I don't need medication. You and I both know that," she stressed. "Anyway, I made a friend. We work together. I'ma be hanging out with her from now on," she said. "So I ain't got time for these damn kids...besides they're always in my got damn way."

Abigail shook her head in disappointment as she listened to her only child. She was not all too fond of the idea of taking care of any babies at her old age, but in all reality they were probably better off with her instead of Ki Ki.

"And what does RJ have to say about all this?" Abigail asked.

Ki Ki paused, and chewed on her bottom lip. It was a nasty habit that she had done for years. "RJ…he um…he left me," she lied.

"Oh my Kiana…"

"Look, ma, I don't wanna talk about that sorry ass nigga," Ki Ki said. "Can I send the damn kids to you or what? If you say no, I'm just gonna drop their asses off at some random orphanage…" She was hoping her mother gave in after hearing that.

"I'll have their flight tickets ready tomorrow," Abigail answered in a weary tone.

***

The following afternoon, Jerrell slowly made his way up the cafeteria line in order to be served the daily slop for the day. On the lunch menu for that afternoon was a bologna sandwich that was nothing more than two slices of white bread with a dry piece of bologna in between. No condiments or nothing. An orange and deserted cake accompanied the meager meal.

Jerrell then wondered if the facility his little brother, Jude was in served better food than the bullshit he was forced to eat just to survive. After collecting his tray, he turned around to head towards his designated table—

Jerrell's food tray suddenly dropped from his hands the moment the blade of a handcrafted shank dug into his abdomen.

CLANK!

The food tray smacked the tile, and his food splattered everywhere.

Jerrell slowly looked down at the blade protruding from his stomach then up into the eyes of the person holding it. Darnell had a menacing look in his eyes as he twisted the blade. Jerrell grunted in pain before spitting up a mouthful of blood.

One of the prisoners quickly noticed what was happening, and shouted out for the guards who rushed over promptly, but not before Darnell viciously stabbed Jerrell in the stomach and chest several more times, slicing into vital organs. He was facing life after a murder and robbery charge, and he figured he pretty much didn't have shit to lose. Darnell felt that his manhood had been insulted after Jerrell had punched him in the rec room.

Before the correction officers could even reach the two, Jerrell collapsed onto the floor. Dark red blood quickly pooled around his body. Darnell had exacted his revenge in the worst possible way imaginable, and unfortunately Jerrell didn't even see the shit coming. Seconds later, his eyes glazed over...

***

"Do ya'll have these in a size seven?" Cameron asked holding up a pair of six inch clear heels. They were sexy, simple, and not too high to dance in.

"Let me check," the cashier smiled. "I love those. I have a pair at home."

Ki Ki stood beside Cameron examining a pair of dominatrix looking leather boots with six inch heels. "How about these?" she held them up.

Cameron took the display shoe from Ki Ki and replaced it on its stand. "Girl, niggas be wanting to see some toes," she said. "Why? Those feet look atrocious?" Cameron teased.

"Never that boo boo," Ki Ki laughed.

Cameron and Ki Ki had used Cam's only free day to go shopping for a couple outfits and dancing shoes at the Ambiance store located in the Southgate Plaza. They wanted to make sure they were on their A game for the private party that weekend. The better they looked, the more tips they'd be able to scrape in.

The bells above the store's door chimed indicating that someone had just entered the store.

The cashier quickly re-emerged from the back room carrying a box of heels. "Hey Keisha," she greeted cheerfully. "Don't worry, I put those red heels in the back for you since I knew you'd be back to get them."

Cameron's gaze slowly wandered over towards the person who had just entered Ambiance. She did an automatic double take at the sight of Pure Seduction. As expected, her trusted sidekick Red was right in tow.

Pure Seduction wore a white fitted tank top and a pair of high waist black leather shorts. On her feet was a pair of cheetah print Christian Louboutins. She had that "I'm the shit and I know it" look on her face that instantly pissed Cameron off.

"Thanks girl," Pure Seduction said. Her gaze then shifted to Cameron and a smile slowly crept across her face. "Well, well, well. Look what the cat dragged in," she teased.

Red giggled.

Cameron shook her head in disbelief. *Here we go,* she thought. "Actually, you're the one who just walked in. So wouldn't you be the triflin' ass cat?" she countered.

Pure Seduction frowned. Her gaze then wandered to the pair of stripper heels in Cameron's hands. "Looks like somebody tryin' to come out of retirement," she joked. "Ya ass done got fired and now you pressed to get back on that pole, huh?"

Cameron waved her off. "Pure, I ain't got time to be trying to entertain your childish ass right now. Come on Ki Ki lets pay for these shoes and get out of here."

Ki Ki followed Cameron to the counter where they purchased the heels, and made their way out of the adult store.

Pure hurriedly purchased the heels she had come to pick out, and made it a mission to catch up to Cameron in the parking lot. She wasn't letting Cameron get off that easily.

"Who is that? Your new lil' friend?" Pure taunted behind Cameron's back. "If it is, aye girl, be careful around that bitch. All of her friends mysteriously die!" Pure and Red broke into a fit of laughter after that comment.

Cameron instantly froze in mid-step.

"Come on. Let's just go," Ki Ki said. "Fuck them corny ass hoes."

Cameron wasn't trying to hear that shit though. Just hearing Pure Seduction make a comment about her deceased friends in the manner she had instantly set her off. Especially since she thought the shit was so amusing.

"Hold this," Cameron said shoving her purse into Ki Ki's hands.

Without another word, she quickly walked up towards Pure Seduction. She still had that stupid ass grin on her face.

"What the fuck you gon' do bitch—"

WHAP!

Cameron punched Pure Seduction dead in the face shutting her ass up once and for all. Pure Seduction's shopping bag dropped onto the pavement after her hands instinctively went up to grab her bloody nose.

Cameron, however, didn't just stop after the first assault. She roughly grabbed Pure Seduction by her Malaysian weave and proceeded to beat the shit out of her right there in the Southgate Plaza parking lot.

"Bitch, I'm so sick of your ass!" Cameron screamed as she pounded her fist into Pure's skull.

She helplessly dropped onto the ground, but Cameron refused to let up dragging her across the parking lot on her knees by her weave. Pure's skin painfully peeled off her knee caps as she was mercilessly dragged across the pavement. She cried out in agony, but even her girl Red was too afraid to jump in, especially since she didn't have a squad of several other dancers to back her up.

Ki Ki stood off to the side holding Cameron's purse as instructed with a sneaky smile on her face. Secretly, she was getting hornier by the second watching Pure Seduction get her ass whupped. Something about violence turned her crazy ass on.

Cameron dragged Pure Seduction towards the nearest car which was a blue metallic Pontiac G6. Slamming her roughly against it, Cameron proceeded to stomp Pure against the vehicle. She was taking out all of her rage on Pure Seduction. All of the pent up anger and frustration Cameron had she was finally releasing on Pure, but she would be damned if she didn't ask for that shit.

The heel of Cameron's studded loafers smashed into Pure Seduction's mouth instantly knocking a couple teeth out. Blood splattered all over her Laverna loafers but she didn't give a damn. She was so sick of Pure Seduction's ass trying her.

Pure fell over onto the ground and began sobbing hysterically. Cameron stared down at her in anger. "You knew better than to keep fucking with me, bitch!" she yelled. "You made me whup your ass again! You should've learned from the ass kicking at Smoove's!"

Cameron's chest heaved up and down as she slowly backed away from Pure Seduction. Several onlookers watched in the distance. Red looked terrified.

"The fuck you looking at hoe?!" Cameron snapped on her.

Red quickly looked away. She didn't want any problems. Instead of retaliating she rushed over to her crying friend's aid.

"Damn, girl," Ki Ki said handing Cameron her purse. "You did that."

"Let's get the hell out of here before I turn around and stomp that hoe some more," Cameron said. Her nostrils flared wildly, and as crazy as she looked she just didn't care. She had lost two close friends, an ex, and the love of her life was behind bars. Aside from her financial issues she had finally had enough. Even the calmest person could snap under the right circumstances.

13

Jude patiently waited for his mother to accept his collect call. In the beginning, every attempt he had made, she'd declined. Jude knew his mother was disappointed in her sons and he couldn't blame her. He had wasted his education, and degree only to be sucked back into a life of crime while running an illegal business.

Eventually she began to accept his calls. After all, she still loved and cared for her sons deeply regardless of the horrible mistakes they had made in life.

Jude was grateful when his mother finally accepted the call. Hearing her voice was music to his ears.

"Hello son," she greeted. Her voice sounded weary and saddened.

"Hey ma...you sound sad," Jude noted. "Is everything good?" he asked in a concerned tone.

His mother paused.

"Ma?" Jude called out. He was unsure if she was even still there.

"No, Jude," she said in a low tone. "Everything is not good..."

"What is it, ma?" Jude asked. "What's going on? You can tell me."

His mother sighed dejectedly. "It's Jerrell," she said in an uneven tone. "It's your brother..."

Jude's stomach instantly knotted up. He was afraid to even ask what was wrong with his brother because he was unsure as to if he actually wanted to hear the answer. "Ma...what happened to Jerrell?" Jude asked.

He could hear the sound of her soft sniffles on the opposite end of the phone, and they instantly made the hairs on the back of his neck stand up.

"I started to write you..." Her voice cracked as she spoke. "But I just couldn't work up the courage to..."

"Ma, what happened to my brother?" There was a hint of anger and excitement in Jude's voice. He wished his mother would just come out, and tell him although he was fearful to actually hear the truth.

"Jerrell...he was killed a couple days ago—"

The receiver dropped out of Jude's hand. Not bothering to pick up the telephone and resume his conversation with his mother, he instead decided to walk away. He couldn't take hearing the shit. As a matter of fact, he didn't even want to believe it.

Jude was escorted back to his prison tier where rec time was currently taking place. He seemed totally out of it as he walked through the sterile white room. Most of the inmates were either playing cards, rapping, or helping one another work out.

Jude didn't seem to notice anything around him as he continued to replay his mother's words over and over again in his mind. Jerrell was Jude's only sibling, so the fact his mother had told him he was gone just seemed unrealistic. Almost as if it was some type of a cruel joke. Jude refused to accept it. He just couldn't.

Jude slowly walked past White's table and headed towards his cell. Fuck rec time. He needed to be alone for a minute. He had to allow the painful realization to sink in because right now he just couldn't accept it.

White snorted. He hated the mere sight of Jude. Truthfully, he was just a racist prick who was angered to see a black man partaking in an operation that only consisted of whites and Mexicans.

"This nigga," White said loud of enough for Jude to hear. The men sitting at the table with him snickered in response.

It was obvious that White simply wanted to get a rise out of Jude. Now, however, wasn't the time for the bullshit.

Jude stopped in his tracks and turned around to face White. "What the fuck you just say?" he asked through gritted teeth.

White smirked, stood to his feet, and rounded the table. He expected everyone in the tier to fear him, but Jude was not that nigga.

He slowly made his way towards Jude and looked down at him disgust. His skin seemed unusually paler than normal. His narrow nostrils flared, and his dark eyes squinted. White was not hiding his blatant hate towards Jude.

"You heard me boy," White said.

WHAP! *WHAP*!

Jude chin-checked his ass twice! White was so stunned, and shocked after the blow that he threw several uncoordinated punches which hit nothing but the air. He stumbled about like a drunken man fighting to keep his balance.

"What was all that shit you were talking?!" Jude barked. "Huh?" He quickly sent a devastating punch to White's jaw before following that up with a right hook to his temple.

White was out for the count before he even hit the floor, landing awkwardly due to his unconsciousness.

Several correctional officers quickly rushed the scene before restraining Jude...

***

Cameron was disappointed when she tried to visit Jude in prison a day after her fight with Pure, but was told that his visitation privileges had been revoked due to disciplinary action. She was really looking forward to venting to him, and hearing some comforting words of wisdom. Her man always knew just the right thing to say to turn any bad situation around.

Jude was the only person in her corner that kept her level-headed, and in return she kept him on the straight and narrow. Jude was the decision-maker, and Cam was the advisor to the decision-maker. That's just how their relationship worked. They balanced one another out.

On the way back to her way house, Cameron received a text message from Marcus that read: *U busy today? Is it cool if I take u to lunch?*

Cameron figured it wasn't much harm in allowing Marcus to treat her to a bite to eat so she went ahead and agreed to it. After showering, and changing her clothes, Marcus picked her up and took her to Cedar Creek Grille. A popular, trendy restaurant located in Beachwood, Ohio.

"You ever been here before?" Marcus asked Cameron once they were seated in their booth.

"No. Never," Cameron answered.

Marcus offered a proud smile. "Cool. I wasn't tryin' to take you nowhere you and ya man already done been," he teased.

Cameron smiled in response.

"But for real though, all jokes aside. I'm really happy you agreed to let me take you to lunch," Marcus said with a charming smile.

Cameron picked up her menu and surveyed it so that she wouldn't get caught up staring into Marcus's sexy eyes. "Well, that's all it is," she said. "Just lunch. Nothin' more."

Marcus scoffed. "Trust me, ain't no engagement ring in my pockets," he joked. "Real talk, I just love your company. I told you from the beginning, that I respect ya relationship...and I really do," he stressed. "But I'm not gon' front like I'm not diggin' you either. I'm just not the type of nigga that's gon' force myself on a female," he said. "I feel when you're ready, you'll come." A smile crept across his thick lips. "And I know you'll be ready...soon enough."

Cameron looked up from her menu and smiled. "Soon enough, huh?" she laughed. "I wouldn't bet on it."

"I would," Marcus said.

"Hmph. You'd lose," she retorted.

"You are so damn pretty," Marcus suddenly said.

Cameron lifted the menu over her face to conceal the fact that she was blushing. She tried to keep it casual wearing a pair of leather leggings, a white sleeveless dress top, and a pair of Alain Quilici wedges. Gold accessories made the outfit pop complemented by a dark red lipstick.

Their waitress suddenly approached their table, and Cameron was very fortunate. The interaction between the two was tensing up, and she had arrived in just the nick of time.

"Can I get you guys started with any beverages or appetizers?" Their waitress asked cheerfully.

"I'll just take a glass of water for now," Cameron ordered.

"Same for me," Marcus said.

"Do you both need a minute to look over the menu?" she asked.

Cameron and Marcus said "Yes" in unison.

After the waitress walked over to fetch their drinks, Marcus resumed the conversation. "So I'm glad we finally got to step out together without me havin' to drop a nigga," he joked.

Cameron vividly remembered the horrible afternoon when Marcus had fought Wallace during their first so called outing together. Embarrassed seemed to be an understatement. Cameron was absolutely mortified. At least fifty percent of the drama in her life involved Wallace's crazy ass.

"You ain't been havin' no problems with that dude again, have you?" Marcus asked in a concerned tone.

"No. I haven't run into Wallace since the last time you saw us together," Cameron answered. And she truly hoped that would be her last run in with him. She was sick and tired of him surfacing when she least expected it.

Marcus looked uncomfortable. "You say it like you know that nigga personally," he noted.

Cameron looked down, and her cheeks flushed in embarrassment. Painful images flooded her mind of him shoving himself inside her against her will. "Trust me, it ain't in the way you think," she said.

Marcus looked relieved. "I was about to say," he joked. "How many niggas I gotta steal you from?"

Cameron shook her head and laughed in amusement.

***

"You mind if I use your restroom?" Marcus asked as he pulled into the driveway of Cameron's luxurious condo.

Cameron tossed him a knowing look. "Yeah...but don't try to be slick," she told him smiling.

Marcus laughed casually. "Me? Slick? Nah, never that," he promised.

After allowing him entrance to her home, Marcus anxiously took in the interior of her place. On the low, he was just trying to see how her man had her living and if he was able to compete. Marcus could be quite competitive even when there was no active competition. Needless to say, Marcus was thoroughly impressed.

"If you're looking for the restroom, it's at the end of the hallway," Cameron said behind him. "Make a left."

Marcus turned around to face Cameron. "Actually I was being slick," he smiled.

Cameron grimaced and folded her arms beneath her breasts. "Why am I not surprised?" she asked.

Marcus suddenly bent down and stole a kiss. He was surprised when Cameron quickly pulled away from the brief kiss.

"Marcus…you know I can't," she whispered.

He ignored her hesitancy and stepped closer. Gently tilting her chin upward, Marcus leaned in for another kiss. Initially, Cameron fought the kiss placing her palms on Marcus's chest in a weak attempt to push him away.

Eventually she gave in, and melted into his body as his warm tongue slid inside her mouth. Marcus slowly removed her hands from his chest, and wrapped her arms around his waist.

Their tongues danced in unison as they indulged in a passion-filled kiss. Suddenly, in one swift movement, Marcus lifted Cameron up. Her legs instinctively wrapped around his waist. Slowly, he walked over towards the nearest wall and gently pressed her back against it. Marcus's rough hands explored the velvet skin of Cameron's back as they sensuously nibbled and sucked on one another's lips.

"Wait, no," Cameron suddenly pulled away. "Marcus, I can't," she said. "I can't do this." Cameron slowly wiggled out of his embrace and onto her feet. "I can't do this with you," she whispered.

Marcus stared at Cameron for several seconds in silence. He was unsure of what her aim was. Was she feeling a nigga or not? Was she simply confused? Was she just afraid to date another male stripper after Silk?

Without thinking clearly, he leaned in for another kiss, but Cameron quickly stopped him. “Marcus…seriously. I cannot do this with you…”

Marcus slowly backed away and nodded his head in understanding. “Aight…I get it,” he said although he truly didn’t.

Marcus was trying to be as patient as he could with Cameron because he truly was digging her, but he also didn’t know why she chose to hold on to something that had long since ended. Her dude was behind bars, and now it was time for the next man to step up to the plate. It may have been selfish but that’s how he honestly felt.

Putting some much needed space between them, Marcus casually strolled through her house until he stopped at her living room accent table. Noticing the faded Polaroid photo, he picked it up. “Who’s this?” he asked staring at the picture of Cameron’s brother.

Cameron quickly walked over, and snatched the photo from Marcus before shoving it inside the drawer of the accent table.

“Who was that?” Marcus wanted to know.

Cameron didn’t respond right away. “My brother…”

“You got a brother?” Marcus asked in disbelief.

“I *had* a brother,” Cameron corrected him.

Marcus regretted pressing the issue. “My bad bay, I ain’t know—”

“It’s cool. It’s cool,” she waved him off.

He cleared his throat suddenly feeling apprehensive. “I guess I’d better gon’ ‘head and get outta here.”

“Yeah...maybe you should,” Cameron agreed.

Marcus slowly leaned down and placed a soft kiss on Cameron’s forehead before heading out.

14

Big Sean's "*Dance*" blared through the speakers of the luxurious two room hotel suite. There were total of six rowdy young guys including Mike, and they had everything a group of college kids could have for entertainment: weed, liquor, great music, and the ultimate entertainment, strippers.

Mike's eyes were glazed over once he opened the hotel door and allowed Cameron and Ki Ki inside. His eyes eagerly scanned their outfits. Both women wore tight fitting Bodycon dresses that hugged every curve of their body.

"Damn, ya'll look good," Mike complemented them as he closed the door.

"You're paying us upfront still right?" Cameron was not beating around the bush. Pocahontas had taught her that shit, and she stuck firmly to the motto: *Get the money first.*

"You know I got you ma," he said before digging in his pocket. He counted each bill off before placing the money in Cameron's hands.

"Give us a few minutes to get ready," Cameron told him.

"Aight then, but don't take too long," Mike said. "Time is money."

"And money is time," Cameron retorted.

Ki Ki followed Cameron towards the bathroom where she closed and locked the door. She then took a seat on the toilet. "Cam, I don't think I can do this shit," she suddenly said.

"What's up? What are you talking about?" Cameron asked.

"These niggas ain't tryin' to see my fat ass dance," Ki Ki said disappointedly.

"Ki Ki, what the hell are you talking about?" she asked. "And what's up with you and all this fat shit? You're thick. It's a big difference," she laughed.

"Seriously, Cameron," Ki Ki said. "I just don't think I can do this shit. At first I was all hype about the money and stuff...but now that I'm here...I guess...I don't know. I'm freezing up," she said. "I'm bitching out."

"All you need is a drink and you'll be fine," Cameron told her. "The first time is always nerve-wracking especially if you don't have any liquor in your system," she explained. "I'ma get you a drink, and you gon' shake that shit off," Cameron said. "Because I really need you here with me. I can't do this shit by myself, and I really need this money Ki Ki," she stressed. As Cameron listened to herself talk she suddenly realized how much she sounded like Pocahontas.

"Well, look...how about you get me that drink first, and then I'll see how I'm feeling afterward," Ki Ki said.

"Alright. You got it," Cameron agreed.

***

Two shots later, Ki Ki's low esteem quickly dissipated as she danced seductively for two of Mike's friends. She was so damn good at what she did, that Cameron could've sworn she had been stripping for years. Ki Ki didn't even seem to mind the men groping her body and fondling her breasts as they sprinkled bills on her large ass.

Travis Porter's "*Get Naked*" played on maximum. Cameron grinded in Mike's lap to the slow melody of the song, and his hands softly caressed her backs as she winded her hips in a circular motion. Mike's erection threatened to burst through the seams of his jeans.

"Turn around. I wanna see that pretty ass face," Mike suddenly said.

Cameron stood to her feet, stepping into a small pile of bills that surrounded her. She then repositioned herself so that she was facing Mike.

"You are so fuckin' bad," he told Cameron. "But I'm sure I ain't tellin' you shit you don't already know. You gotta lucky ass dude at home, don't you?"

"Maybe...maybe not," Cameron teased. She would tell a guy just what he wanted to hear in a heartbeat. One of the hallmarks of being a great hustler.

"How you feel about tryin' to make some extra money," Mike suddenly offered. "Just me and you," he hinted.

Plies *"Ms Pretty Pussy"* suddenly began playing on the mixtape Mike had put together.

Cameron wasn't crazy about the idea of turning tricks. She was usually content with the tips she made, and she didn't do anything besides a little grinding here and a little flirtation there. Sex was personal, and in her opinion meant to be shared with someone she truly cared about. Not to be sold for the right price.

"I ain't with turnin' no tricks," Cameron admitted.

Mike chuckled, and his cute dimples were on full display. "First of all, I ain't no trick baby girl," he said. "And second of all, why you gotta look at it like that?" he asked. "You here to make money, right? And, shit, I'm here to spend it. Why not help each other out?"

Cameron couldn't believe she was actually toying with the idea after all the shit she had talked to Pocahontas about selling her body.

"Just name the price," Mike said.

Cameron shook her head. "Sorry, I'm not for sale," she told him.

"Shit, everything's got a price," Mike said.

Silence.

"Five hundred?" was Mike's first offer.

Silence.

"A stack..."

Silence.

"Come on Cameron," Mike said. "Say something...you're in school just like me. Hell, we need all the money we can get. School fees can be a bitch, right?" It was almost as if he was reading Cameron's pockets and knew she was in desperate need of the cash.

Finally swallowing her pride, she said, "Fifteen hundred..."

Mike whistled sarcastically. "Damn, ma," he laughed. "You tryin' to clean a nigga out, ain't you?"

Cameron shrugged. "School fees can be a bitch, right?" she repeated.

Mike nodded his head in admiration. "I can do that," he finally agreed. He slowly picked Cameron up and placed her on her feet. Grabbing her by the hand, he guided her towards the nearest bedroom.

Ki Ki was on her hands and knees popping her ass in the center of the living room. Bills rained down on her, and she was so in her zone that she didn't even seem to notice Cameron leaving.

Once inside the bedroom, Mike closed and locked the bedroom door. Cameron's stomach flipped and churned. She may as well have been selling her soul to the devil.

I said I would never do this shit, a part of her said.

But you need this money, the other side of her said.

Cameron felt as if she had an angel on one shoulder, while the devil lingered on the other.

"Don't just stand there, come over here…" Mike slowly climbed into the bed and pulled his t-shirt over his head exposing his toned bare chest.

Cameron's heart thumped louder with each step she took. "Do you…um…want me to take my clothes off?" she stammered. Her throat felt dry, and her hands were clammy. She tried to push Jude to the back of her mind.

Mike chuckled. "Nah, I want you to keep that shit on," he said in a sarcastic tone. "Hell yeah, I want you to take that off. I wanna see that pussy."

Mike licked his full lips as Cameron took her time stepping out of her black slingshot bikini. "Damn…" He eyed her shaved kitty. "Come here," he patted the space beside him.

Cameron swallowed the large lump that had formed in her throat as she slowly made her way over towards the king size bed. The mattress squeaked a little as she crawled over towards him.

Mike's hands slid up and down Cameron's nude body. "Loosen up," he whispered.

Mike's left hand gently spread her thighs apart. He leaned down towards Cameron, and placed soft kisses on her neck. Her body tensed up even more then, because she was trying so hard not to enjoy the sensation of his breath tickling her skin.

Mike slipped a finger inside of her pussy. Cameron instantly stiffened although Mike had told her several times to just relax.

You need this money, she constantly repeated to herself.

Mike slipped his finger out and sucked off her juices. "Mmm. You taste sweet," he said. He leaned in preparing to kiss Cameron, but she quickly turned her head away avoiding the kiss.

In a sudden fit of rage, Mike grabbed her by the cheeks, and forced her face towards him before jamming his tongue in her mouth. He damned near forced his long tongue down her throat. His nails dug into the skin of her cheeks. Once he felt satisfied with the forceful kiss, he flung her head away.

Mike looked frustrated but still determined to get some pussy. He slowly lowered himself to her supple breasts and popped a hardened brown nipple inside his mouth. Apparently, Mike was the only one enjoying what he was doing as he emitted soft moans.

Cameron's jaw muscle tensed as she stared unblinkingly at the ceiling. Mike slowly reached down to touch her pussy again, and Cameron quickly slapped his hand away that time.

Mike looked at Cameron like she was crazy. "Bitch, whatchu' really tryin' to do 'cause I ain't got time to play no mothafuckin' games."

Cameron slowly got up and climbed out the bed—Mike quickly grabbed her wrist and stared at her menacingly. "Why the fuck you agree to do this shit if you were gonna act like this?!" he yelled.

Cameron snatched her arm away from Mike. The look she gave him caused an unsettling feeling in the pit of his stomach.

Mike sucked his teeth in disgust. "Gon' get the fuck on, bitch," he said in a dismissive tone.

Cameron quickly exited the room, and hurried into the bathroom where she promptly redressed. Ki Ki didn't miss the awkwardness of the situation as she made her way into the bathroom seconds after. Cameron was pulling her dress on by then.

"Where the hell are you going?" Ki Ki asked confused. Beads of sweat were on her forehead, but she was having the time of her life drinking, partying, and making money. She had never had so much fun.

"I'm leaving," Cameron said. "And if you aren't trying to get left, then I suggested you hurry up and get dressed too," she said in a serious tone.

"What the fuck is up with you?" Ki Ki asked. "You actin' all crazy all of a sudden. And why I gotta leave just because you don't wanna stay. That's fucking up my money, ain't it?"

Cameron grabbed her purse, and pulled the strap over her shoulder. “Suit yourself,” she said nonchalantly heading out the bathroom.

Ki Ki quickly stepped in Cameron’s way blocking her exit. “Why you acting all stuck up and shit when you know you need the money?” she asked. “Ain’t that what you said earlier?”

“Fuck the money, and fuck you,” Cameron said coolly. She then pushed her way past Ki Ki and practically ran out of the hotel.

Once she made it outside, she vomited in the parking lot. Cameron had never felt so disgusted and disappointed in herself.

***

“Damn…what happened to your girl?” one of Mike’s friends asked Ki Ki.

“I don’t know,” she answered. “I guess she wasn’t feeling the party…”

Mike suddenly emerged from the bedroom smoking a Black & Mild. There was a look of irritation on his handsome face. His eyes narrowed as he stared at Ki Ki intensely as if he were looking at her for the first time ever.

“Well, you still gon’ stay and entertain us, right?” Mike asked. “I mean, shit, a nigga just broke bread on ya’ll asses and ya girl ran outta here and left us hangin’.”

"I don't know," Ki Ki answered apprehensively. "Maybe I'd better get my ass out of here too. I only agreed to do this since Cam and I were doing it together—"

"Shit, we can take care of you," one of Mike's friends cut her off.

"Yeah, you in good hands," another piped up.

"All I know is I just spent over two stacks on this mothafuckin' party and I ain't even havin' no fun," Mike said.

"Yeah, I think it's time to turn this shit up," one of his friends agreed. "Let's have some fun with this bitch."

Ki Ki didn't like the way they were eyeing her. She was a tough girl, and usually able to hold her own, but with six grown ass men there wasn't too much she could do to defend herself.

"Ya'll sound like ya'll on some other shit," Ki Ki tossed her hands up. "I'm getting the fuck outta here—"

Suddenly, one of Mike's friends grabbed her before she could walk off. Initially, everything seemed like fun and games, but now shit had gotten real—and violent too as she was slapped around the living room. The blows came so quick and suddenly that she didn't know which of the guys had hit her. Before she knew it, she was lying on the ground wiping away the blood pouring from the cut on her bottom lip.

One of Mike's drunken friends unzipped his pants and pulled his dick out. "Aye ya'll check this out," he said.

A stream of urine shot out the tip of his dick as he aimed at Ki Ki. "Hit the target, win a prize!" He laughed at his own crude humor. Urine splashed onto Ki Ki's bare thigh.

"Come on, man, chill!" Mike yelled. "I'm tryin' to fuck. I ain't gon' be able to hit no pissy ass pussy!" he snapped.

"Get the fuck away from her!"

Everyone turned their attention towards Cameron who was standing in the doorway aiming her 9mm at them. They would have found the shit amusing had she not cocked the Glock. The expression on her face was that of a serious one. She was not fucking around at all.

"Come on, Ki Ki," she said in an authoritative tone. As bad as she wanted to leave her ass there for not leaving earlier, Cameron couldn't turn her back on her. Hell, that was how she had gotten raped during a so called private party.

Ki Ki scurried to her feet, and collected all the singles off the living room floor. Cameron rolled her eyes in irritation. "Ki Ki, come on," she repeated.

"Ya'll ratchet ass hoes on some other shit," Mike said shaking his head.

"I wouldn't be talking that shit if I were you," Cameron threatened.

"I was just tryin' to put some money in *your* pocket," he stressed.

"Yeah, but beating and pissing on us wasn't a part of the deal," she said.

Mike grimaced. "What can I say?" he asked. "We get a lil' wild sometimes. It's all in fun."

"Fuck you," Cameron spat.

Ki Ki grabbed her belongings, and she and Cameron quickly left the hotel room.

"Are you alright?" Cameron asked Ki Ki as they sped walked towards the elevators. She looked over her shoulder every few seconds fearful that Mike and his boys would burst through the door in an attempt to purse them.

"I'm fine," Ki Ki answered. As scared as she was of the men beating her senseless somewhere in the back of her mind, she also liked the shit...

15

Cameron was anxious to see Jude the second time she drove up to the correctional facility. Her excitement, however, quickly faded after she was told that he refused his visit. His visiting privileges had returned, but he just flat out refused to see her. Cameron felt a combination of hurt and confusion. She wasn't expecting to hear that, and she really was looking forward to seeing him and talking to him.

As funny as it may have seemed, Cameron even thought out the entire conversation in her head on the drive to the prison. She couldn't wait to tell him about the fight with Pure Seduction, and how school was going so far. She had no intention of telling him about the private party, but now that she was deprived of seeing him it wasn't like he would know either way. Cameron couldn't figure out why he would just flat out refuse to see her.

Did I do something wrong?

Is he upset with me?

Does he know about the abortion appointment?

Don't be stupid, Cameron. He couldn't possible know about the appointment, she told herself.

Whatever the reason was for Jude refusing to see her she wished he would at least call and let her know why. After all, communication was the key to a successful relationship.

Saddened and disappointed, Cameron prepared for her lengthy drive back home. She just prayed that whatever Jude was going through he'd be okay.

***

Jude lay in the top bunk of his bed and stared at the ceiling of his prison cell. He couldn't eat. He couldn't sleep. He didn't want to talk to or see anyone including his girl. Jude was in a state of solitaire as he tried his best to cope with his loss.

How am I going to live my life without my brother in my corner, he asked himself repeatedly.

All of his life it had just been him and Jerrell. Jerrell had helped mold Jude into the man he was today. Hell, if it wasn't for Jerrell he would have never met Cameron.

Jude was completely grief-stricken, and confused about how to go about going on to the next important step which was letting go. Instead he was pushing his loved ones away while trying to deal with the pain on his own. Little did he know that strategy would actually hurt him more than help him.

***

Jude strolled casually through the courtyard the following afternoon. It was the closest thing the inmates came to getting a breath of fresh air. Most prisoners entertained themselves with a game of basketball, others stayed busy by exercising, while the rest conversed.

Jude kicked a nearby pebble while lost in his own thoughts. He had barely said more than two words to his own roommate, and honestly he just wanted to be left the hell alone. His gaze wandered over towards a group of inmates doing a vigorous workout routine together.

Suddenly, Jude heard the rapid sound of footsteps approach him from behind! Before he could even turn all the way around, a closed fist quickly connected with his jaw. Jude instantly lost his balance and crashed onto the concrete.

Inmates immediately stopped what they were doing in order to see what the hell was going on.

White and two of his boys proceeded to viciously stomp and kick Jude while he lay helplessly on the ground, shielding his face and head from the devastating blows. His torso and legs took a major beating, and he was certain that one of his ribs may have been fractured.

Unfortunately, he had been caught slipping instead of watching his back. That was the number one rule or prison.

Every part of Jude's body was a target for White and his goons as they continued to violently stomp out Jude. None of the other inmates bothered to step in, and stop the madness. After all, no one wanted to get involved in someone else's drama.

Jude suddenly tried to grab White's leg in a desperate attempt to make him fall over, but that proved to be a big mistake. The bottom of White's shoe connected with Jude's head which bounced off the concrete immediately knocking him unconscious…

***

The minute Cameron returned home from the prison, she checked her mailbox for the bills that were bound to be there. After sifting through the electric bill, water bill, and her cellphone bill, she noticed a letter that she had received from the Cuyahoga Department Corrections Facility.

A smile slowly crept across her face because she knew that it was from Jude. However, her smile quickly disappeared when she wondered why he had chosen to mail her a letter only to turn around and refuse her visit. After further scrutinizing the letter, she noticed that the handwriting on the letter didn't seem to match Jude's at all.

Cameron hoped for the best but expected the worst as she made her way inside her condo. She decided to go ahead, and open the letter the minute she stepped inside the foyer. Carefully, she removed the folded piece of notebook paper. She expected to see a hand-written letter but instead was greeted with the disappointing sight of a blank paper, and inside of that a Green Dot Pre-paid card.

Jude had gotten up with a trusted CO that he paid to put his earned money on the Pre-paid card. He then instructed him to mail it off to the address given. It wasn't much, but it was all he had in order to help her out financially.

Cameron's cheeks quickly flushed in anger. "Why would he send me this bullshit, and then turn around and not even see me during visitation. What the fuck is he on?" she asked herself.

In a sudden fit of rage, she placed the meaningless Pre-paid card into the envelope and tossed it inside the drawer of the of the accent table on top of the picture of her deceased brother. Cameron hated trying to figure people out, and she was frustrated that she was unable to try to even figure out what Jude was on.

I wish that I could have this moment for life…

'Cause in this moment I just feel so alive…

Cameron's cellphone rang in her purse. She dug into her purse and answered the call. "Hello?"

"Hey, Cam. What's up girl? It's Ki Ki," she greeted cheerfully.

Cameron wished her mood matched Ki Ki's but unfortunately it didn't. Instead she felt a combination of irritation, confusion, and disappointment.

"Hey, girl. Just getting in the house," Cameron told her. "What's up?"

Ki Ki sounded like she was inside of a car. "So, look I know the first lil' private party we did didn't go as planned, but on some real shit, I love the money we made," she admitted. "It was fast, convenient, and right on time. You know? On the real, I'm trying to get some money like that again. Damn this bartending gig," she said.

Cameron thought about what Ki Ki was saying. She had promised Jude that she was done with the stripper lifestyle, but she had already broken her promise when she agreed to do the private party with Mike.

Anyway Jude seemed to be on whatever he was on, so Cameron decided that she could play the same type of game. "Fuck it," she said. "I'm down too..."

16

Daggers was a popular hood after hour spot located off Miles Rd. After Smoove's closed down this was pretty much the spot that everyone migrated to for late night entertainment. It was the type of place where anything went down, and although it could indeed get pretty rowdy there were some ballers who frequented the club on a regular basis.

"You ever danced here before?" Ki Ki asked as Cameron pulled into the broken up gravel that served as the small club's driveway.

"No. But I've danced at after hour spots before. Trust me, there's money to be made," Cameron told her. She didn't dare want to go into details about the fact that she'd also been raped, and witnessed one of her best friends get murdered in after hour spots.

Cameron parked her truck in an empty space and turned off the engine. She was just about to step out her vehicle, when Ki Ki suddenly grabbed her wrist.

"Wait, Cam," she said. "I gotta ask you something that's been on my mind."

Cameron closed the driver's door and relaxed in her seat. "What's that?" she asked.

Ki Ki drew in a deep breath and released it. "That day when you fought that chick in the parking lot," she began. "What did she mean when she said 'be careful around you because all you friends die'?"

Cameron figured the question would arise sooner or later so she wasn't surprised. Hell, if the shoe was on the other foot she'd ask Ki Ki the exact same question. "That bitch was just being stupid," Cameron answered. "Don't feed into that shit."

Ki Ki nodded her head. "Well, I knew she had to just be talking shit," she said. "You seem like a damn good friend. Especially since you came back for me at the hotel and all. Shit, I don't know what those niggas would've did to me if you hadn't come back," Ki Ki told her.

Cameron shrugged it off. "We gotta have each other's backs," she said. "Now you ready to go in here and get this money?"

"You know it."

Daggers was pretty crowded that night. It was a BYOB type of place so almost every guy in the place had a bottle or beer in his hand. The place was set up much like a club on the inside. There was a spacious dance floor in the center of the room and lined along each wall of the club were several booths which all happened to be occupied.

In the center of the dance floor was a metallic pole. Cameron did a double take when she noticed Juicy doing her thing on stage. She hadn't seen her since she last worked at The Shakedown.

People were posted on the walls and there were a couple fellas playing pool in the farthest corner of the club.

The lights were always dimmed inside of Daggers and it was that way for a reason. Anything and everything went down in that place from the dancers fucking in the booths for the right price, to the fellas hitting licks and trying to earn a dollar. It was just that type of spot.

"You nervous?" Cameron shouted over the music to be heard. "If you nervous we don't gotta stay," she said.

Ki Ki watched a flurry of bills rain down on Juicy as she slid down from the metallic pole into a full blown split position, and began humping the stage in a seductive manner.

Ki Ki turned to face Cameron. "Are you crazy?" she asked. "This is just my kinda spot!"

"Well come on. Let's go get dressed."

Ki Ki followed Cameron towards the dressing room. Inside had to be over fifteen dancers prepping for their upcoming performances. A few were smoking weed, and some were even cleaning their kitties so they'd be fresh when they sold it to the highest bidder in the club. Those were the types of females that were all about their money, and didn't give a damn how and what they had to do to get it. Although, it wasn't Cameron's cup of tea, she had no choice but to respect it. At the end of the day they were all hustlers.

"Oh, goodness. Don't tell me it's more hoes coming in here," one of the dancers complained as she watched Cameron and Ki Ki file into the dressing room.

Cameron tossed the woman a nasty stare. "I don't know about any hoes, but if you mean dancers then yeah. We're in here trying to get money just like you."

The woman rolled her eyes, but didn't respond.

"Damn. Are all strippers bitchy like that?" Ki Ki whispered.

Cameron began pulling her outfit and shoes out of her rolling suitcase. "Women just hate competition period," she answered not looking at Ki Ki. "And that's all we are to each other pretty much. The more females…the more competition."

"Is it like that in the actual strip clubs?" Ki Ki asked.

Cameron snorted. "It's worse," she said.

Cameron taught Ki Ki how to work the floor by getting lap dances and flirting with guys for tips. With a roster full of strippers no one was guaranteed a turn to go up on stage, and there was always the possibility that you wouldn't get "rained" on so you had to make it do what it do by working the floor to your advantage. Luckily, the two ended up going on stage after the stuck up rude chick in the dressing room. They actually decided to go up together. Mainly because Ki Ki was afraid and nervous to go up alone. Secondly, because they would probably clean up twice as much on the tip side if they performed together. The two could split the tips fifty-fifty.

Ki Ki worked her end of the stage while Cameron worked the opposite end. Suddenly, Cameron watched as the last face she expected to see approached the stage with a small wad of bills in his hand and a wide grin on his chubby face.

Cameron purposely walked away from Wallace not even bothering to provide him with any up close and personal interaction. Instead she walked over towards the other men who were standing and waiting to tip her.

Once their turn on stage was up, Cameron rushed Ki Ki to hurry up and get dressed so they could leave, but Ki Ki was not trying to hear that shit once again.

"Cameron, it's so much money to be made in here still," Ki Ki argued. "Why are we running out? You said so yourself that we'd clean up working the floor? You're going to let all these other hoes get our money?"

Cameron couldn't stand the thought of being in the same exact setting as Wallace. Every time she laid eyes on him she wanted to get as far away from him as possible.

"Ki Ki, you wouldn't understand—"

"We're friends, right Cameron?" Ki Ki demanded to know.

Cameron nodded her head.

"Then tell me."

Cameron exhaled in frustration. She never told a soul about what Wallace did to her the night Pocahontas and Juicy left her at the strange home in Columbus.

"Did you see the fat ass dude with braids that came up to the stage to tip us?" Cameron asked.

"The one you walked away from?" Ki Ki asked. "Yeah.Why?"

"Well...he...attacked me a few months ago," Cameron admitted. She couldn't bear to say the word raped.

"Attacked you?!" Ki Ki repeated. "What do you mean attacked you?"

Cameron gave Ki Ki a knowing look. "Please don't make me say it," she pleaded.

Ki Ki's eyes bulged in their sockets. "I would've killed his ass if he had done that shit to me," she said.

Little did Cameron know, Ki Ki was dead ass serious. "We've ran into each other a few times after the incident, and every time he makes it his mission to fuck with me," Cameron said. "So now do you understand why I want to leave?" she asked.

"Yeah," Ki Ki answered. "I do..."

She followed Cameron into the dressing room where they promptly dressed and headed out towards the parking lot. Cameron walked hastily towards her truck, and pulled out her car keys—

CLINK!

Cameron's car keys dropped from her hands and landed on the gravel. She was totally caught off guard by the sight of Wallace leaning against her driver door. He was leaning against her shit like he had purchased it. Obviously, he had been waiting for her.

"You just love fucking with me. Don't you?" Cameron asked in irritation.

"It's too much fun," Wallace answered smugly.

He was so into Cameron that he didn't even notice Ki Ki standing on the opposite end of Cameron's trunk. As a matter of fact, he didn't even know that the two had come together.

"So I see you ain't wanna dance for a nigga on stage," Wallace noted. "What? First you turned down my drink now my money ain't good enough for you either?"

"You need help," Cameron said in disgust.

He laughed. "Nah, I need some pussy," he corrected her.

Cameron backed up as Wallace made his way towards her. "I never get tired of this cat and mouse shit," he said. "I could do this—"

His sentence immediately trailed off after Ki Ki jammed the blade of her Harley Davidson pocketknife into the side of Wallace's neck.

"*Uurgghh*!" he groaned in pain.

Ki Ki quickly snatched the knife out of Wallace's neck and backed away. The knife had once belonged to RJ, but obviously the weapon was useless to him now that he was rotting away in the woods.

Blood spurted out of Wallace's neck similar to CG effects, only this shit was the real deal. A look of fear and panic was etched on his feet as he grabbed his neck in an attempt to stop the rapid blood flow. He uncontrollably fell against Cameron's truck before tumbling to the ground.

Gurgling noises came from his throat as he choked and spat up his own blood. Ki Ki casually wiped his blood off the knife onto her leather jacket.

"Ki Ki," Cameron said in a low tone. "What did you do?"

"He was about to try to hurt you," Ki Ki defended herself. "You said we gotta have each other's backs, right?" she asked.

Cameron didn't respond as she stared down at Wallace in horror. The gurgling noises had quickly ceased, and he was now completely motionless. His glazed over eyes were staring up at the star-filled sky.

Wallace was dead.

"Ki Ki...what did you do?" Cameron repeated. She was in total shock and disbelief about what had just taken place in a matter of seconds.

"Would you stop asking that stupid shit?!" Ki Ki snapped. "Help me get his body in the trunk before anyone comes out. We can't just leave his ass here."

Cameron slowly looked up at Ki Ki, and for the first time, she realized that she truly didn't know this chick.

Why do I ever try to be friends with females, she asked herself.

17

"Pull over right here," Ki Ki instructed.

Cameron slowly eased her truck to a stop alongside Turner Rd. If it wasn't for the few street lights illuminating the downhill road it would have been pitch black.

"Put the blinkers on just in case," Ki Ki said.

Cameron did as she was instructed.

"Come on let's hurry up and get this shit done with," Ki Ki told Cameron.

Cameron seemed out of it as she climbed out the truck and rounded the vehicle. She opened the trunk and Wallace's limp arm fell out. Great. Cameron would be scrubbing the trunk for days in order to get all the blood out.

"Come on. Help me get him out," Ki Ki said.

Cameron may have been tripping, but it seemed like Ki Ki was a little too relaxed about everything almost as if this wasn't her first time doing this shit.

Together they carried his body deep off into the woods near the side of the road. The task was anything but easy considering Wallace's weight.

"Fat fuck," Ki Ki complained.

Cameron sniffed the air around her and made a face in disgust. "What is that smell?" she asked.

Ki Ki smelled it too, and she knew exactly what the putrid odor was. It was the smell of RJ's body decomposing a few yards from where they stood.

"I don't know," Ki Ki lied. "Maybe a dead deer or some shit. Don't worry about it. Let's just hurry up and drop this fat ass nigga and get the hell out of here."

***

"Are you mad at me?" Ki Ki asked once she and Cameron were back inside the truck.

Cameron sat motionless in the driver's seat as she stared straight ahead. The sound of her blinkers clicked repeatedly as they sat on the side of the road. Her hands were covered in Wallace's blood, and all she could think about was the look in his eyes after Ki Ki had brutally stabbed him.

"Cameron...Are you mad at me?" Ki Ki repeated in a concerned tone.

Cameron turned to face Ki Ki. "It's not about me being mad at you," she said. "Dude, you just killed a man..."

"You act like we just killed some innocent ass nigga—"

"We?!" Cameron repeated. "*You* stabbed him. I didn't do shit," she corrected her.

Ki Ki smiled. "Whatever you say to make you sleep at night, Cameron," she said. "But you and I both know that he would've never stopped if someone hadn't stopped him."

***

Jude stepped into Stone's cell the following afternoon during rec time. "You wanted to see me?" he asked. Both of his eyes were blackened, and there was a nasty bruise on the left side of his head. White and his boys had been removed from the general population due to their actions.

Stone sighed. "Yeah. I do," he answered. He picked up his pack of cigarettes and offered Jude one. "Cigarette?"

Jude could definitely use a smoke after the L he took yesterday so he gladly accepted. "Good lookin'."

"I don't want you apart of my operation any longer," Stone suddenly said.

"Look, if this about ya boy White he started that shit with me," Jude said. "He ain't been feelin' me since day one—"

"This ain't got nothing to do with White," Stone interrupted him.

"Then what is it? I been doin' everything you told me to do and haven't been caught slippin' not once. I told you I'ma hustler. The shit is in me." Jude patted his chest.

Stone sighed in frustration. “You know what?” he asked. “I see something in you that I saw in myself once,” he said. “You’re a good kid. I don’t want you mixed up in my shit.”

Jude sighed in frustration. “But I need this work for my girl and my baby,” he said. “These pennies they pay us in here ain’t gon’ do shit for me.”

Stone nodded in agreement. “I know,” he said. “And that’s why I plan on lookin’ out for you. Anything you need, I got you. You hear me?”

Jude breathed a sigh of relief. He wasn’t expecting to hear that, but he was totally grateful for it.

“And don’t worry about White,” he added. “I’ll have a talk with him when he gets back in general population. Make sure he doesn’t try any stupid shit like that again,” he promised.

“I really appreciate that, man,” Jude said.

“My ass is never getting out of here,” Stone told him. “I don’t have shit to lose...but you do...”

***

Days quickly turned into weeks since Jude had last spoken to or seen Cameron. In the beginning, he was simply pushing her away in order to mourn the loss of his brother, but now he was actually beginning to believe that she deserved more than what he could offer to her behind bars.

Jude figured it would be selfish to make her wait for him when he was the one who had gotten himself in the mess he was in. However, he still continued to send her money via a trusted correction officer. Unbeknownst to Jude, every letter he sent to Cameron was shoved into a drawer and never even opened for that matter.

Cameron was beginning to come to the realization that what she and Jude had was slowly dissipating. He refused her visits, and never even called. She was beginning to feel like Jude was only sending those bullshit ass cards out of obligation, and every time she received a letter from him she began to despise him more and more.

Cameron wasn't some fucking charity case. The fact that she had the courage to take her clothes off just to make a dollar showed that she wasn't afraid to do what she had to do to survive. She didn't need some punk ass pre-paid cards she needed the love, attention, and affection that any woman craved for in a relationship

Jude had wanted Cameron to hold him down during his time of need, and she did. However, it was funny that he was the one who was actually turning his back on her. She felt hurt and confused.

Cameron's thoughts were suddenly interrupted when her cellphone rang. Grabbing her phone off the coffee table in front of her, she scanned the caller ID.

"What's up," she answered.

"You," Marcus simply said.

"What about me?"

"I wanna see you..."

Cameron had been trying to keep her distance from Marcus lately out of the loyalty and love she had for Jude, but now he was treating her like he didn't want her in his corner anymore. He never called. Every time she went to the prison, he denied her visits, and he didn't even have enough decency to write her a damn letter to explain his strange behavior. Evidently, he was pushing her way to the point of no return.

Right about now she was ready to do some shit that she would never be able to take back just to spite Jude. As petty as it seemed, that was just how she felt.

"When?" Cameron asked.

18

"I would've never thought you could cook, Marcus," Cameron said sarcastically.

She sat comfortably on his cozy Glencrest sofa in his living room. Marcus lived in a four bedroom two bathroom home in a quiet cul de sac located in South Euclid, Ohio. He had just recently moved there from the west side of Cleveland, and it was his first home. Marcus had been making some major moves with the money he earned making sure to invest in the right things.

Marcus stepped into the living room, and handed Cameron a small glass of wine. "What you tryin' to say? 'Cuz a nigga dance, I'm not gon' be able to cook," he joked.

Cameron laughed. "You said that. I didn't."

"Yeah, you sure weren't complaining about it either," he teased taking a seat beside her on the sofa.

Marcus had prepared creamy Cajun chicken pasta. Needless to say, Cameron was thoroughly pleased with his skills, and shocked to say the very least.

"I am happy and surprised you even came over here...," Marcus said. "Told you it'd only be a matter of time before you're mine. I've been breakin' ya lil' ass down slowly but surely," he joked.

"I'm not yours," Cameron quickly said in a sarcastic tone.

"Well, you ain't that nigga's either 'cuz you over here with me right now," Marcus said confidently. He had done a line of cocaine before Cameron even came over, and he was feeling himself a little more than usual.

Cameron cut her eyes at Marcus. A smirk played in the corners of her mouth. "Whatever," she said casually before taking a small sip of wine.

"It's quiet as hell in here," Marcus suddenly said. "Let me turn on some music." He stood to his feet and walked over towards the entertainment console.

Seconds later, Trey Songz' soulful voice filled the room as his single "*You Belong to Me*" played softly.

"So I didn't know that you and Pure Seduction had something special going on between ya'll," Cameron said over the music.

Marcus made his way over towards her. "Keyword...*had*," he said flatly. "She ain't relevant to me."

Cameron rolled her eyes sarcastically. "Yeah right," she disagreed.

"You the only woman I give a fuck about," he said. "Anybody else is nonexistent. Period point blank."

"I hear you," Cameron said sarcastically.

"I wish you could say the same about me..."

"Hmm...wish I could too..."

Marcus chuckled. "You're so cold, Cameron," he said. "I kinda like that shit though," he admitted. "I can appreciate a challenge." He stood directly in front of her, slowly grabbed both her hands, and placed them around his firm waist.

Marcus did a sensuous dance that probably got the women in the male revue going crazy. However, all it did was make Cameron burst out laughing. Marcus burst into a fit of laughter seconds after.

"Boy, you are so crazy," Cameron laughed.

Marcus's humorous expression quickly turned into a sensual one as he stared at Cameron with lust-filled eyes. He slowly got down onto his knees and positioned himself between her legs. "Damn…I been diggin' you for so long, Cam," he said.

Slowly leaning inward, Marcus brushed his soft lips over Cameron's. Her legs wrapped around his torso as she gave in to the passionate kiss, tossing her arms around his neck in the midst of it.

Marcus wasted no time as he lifted Cameron, and stood to his feet. His strong hands cradled her soft butt cheeks in the high waist acid wash leggings she wore. Her legs were wrapped firmly around his waist. Slowly, he made his way towards his bedroom all the while kissing and sucking Cameron's lips.

Once Marcus made it inside his master bedroom, he carefully laid Cameron down on his king size bed, and gently climbed on top of her.

"I want you," he said in between kisses. "But I'll be damned if I'ma share you."

"You won't have to," Cameron said in a low tone.

Just hearing her say those words felt like music to his ears. He'd been waiting forever just to hear her finally say that.

"Don't tell me that shit if you don't mean it..."

Cameron pulled Marcus's head down and eagerly crushed her lips against his. After they pulled apart to catch their breaths, he proceeded to slowly undress her. Cameron's breath caught in her chest as she watched Marcus lower his face towards her waist. This time they weren't at Pandora's Box, and he wasn't performing. This was the real deal.

"*Ooohh,*" she whimpered as him warm mouth closed over her sopping pussy.

His thick, pink tongue licked and sucked on her pearl. Cameron's back arched in response, and her toes curled.

"You mine now. You hear me?" Marcus asked as he climbed on top of her.

Cameron bit her bottom lip seductively and nodded her head. Feeling satisfied with her response, he slid inside her tight walls.

"*Ooohh,*" she moaned.

"Take your dick," Marcus whispered in Cameron's ear.

With each stroke he delivered, she got wetter by the second. Marcus's strokes were deep and slow. He wanted to fuck Cameron to the point where she'd forget all about the love she had for Jude.

"You mine now," he repeated. "I ain't gon' let ya ass go either..."

19

One Year and Six Months Later.

"Happy birthday to my god son!" Ki Ki sang. She began placing kisses all over Cameron's son's face including his lips. He was more concerned with the wrapped present in Ki Ki's hands than returning her affection.

"Ki Ki, what did I tell you about kissing my child all in his mouth?" Cameron asked. "Xavier, did you see Marcus? He was supposed to have ordered the pizza?" she asked in an irritated tone.

Trying to host a birthday party for a one year old at Chuck E. Cheese was definitely proving to be a lot of work. Cameron could barely keep up with the dozens of kids Marcus had invited from his side of the family. All of the adults invited seemed to be too preoccupied with their own affairs to help out in the least.

It was mighty funny how people begged to be invited to a party, but couldn't even offer the slightest assistance.

"I think he went to the bathroom," Xavier said before walking off to flirt with the single mother he had been scoping for the last ten minutes.

Cameron tossed her hands up in frustration. "Seems like I gotta do everything my damn self—Ki Ki, please stop kissing my son on his mouth?" she said in a weary tone.

"What?" Ki Ki asked defensively. "He's just so cute. I can't help it," she cooed.

Cameron walked over towards Ki Ki, and took her son from her before she ended up having to slap her. Ki Ki was the best god mother a woman could ask for though. She was even there when Cameron gave birth to Justin a year ago. They had become closer than sisters, never once speaking about the dark, painful night that Wallace had been murdered. Kiki had been there for her graduation, and even helped Cameron run the new boutique that she'd gotten, courtesy of Marcus's investment.

Justin immediately began whining after Cameron deprived him of opening the gift Ki Ki had just given him.

"After you open your eat," she told him. "Where's your daddy at?"

As if on cue, Marcus emerged from the public restroom and made his way over towards his family.

Cameron released a sigh of relief. "There you are, Marcus. I asked you..." Her voice instantly trailed off when she noticed a small amount of white residue on the tip of Marcus's nose.

"What?" Marcus asked dumbfounded.

Cameron pointed to her own nose gesturing that he had something on his, although unfortunately she knew exactly what that *something* was. Throughout their relationship, Marcus had been battling a cocaine addiction that only seemed to grow worse as the days progressed.

Marcus quickly wiped away the powdery substance on his nose before any of his relatives saw it—not that they weren't already aware of his drug addiction.

Cameron rolled her eyes in irritation, and walked away. He had promised her two weeks ago that he was done with the shit, only to turn around and use it on their son's birthday, and inside of a Chuck E. Cheese restroom of all places.

So many times Cameron considered leaving Marcus due to his nasty drug problem, but the fact of the matter was she loved the family life she had grown accustomed to. She didn't want to give that up as foolish as it may have seemed.

***

"Why you so quiet?" Marcus asked in the car on their ride home from Chuck E. Cheese. "You mad or some shit?"

Cameron didn't respond. Instead she rolled her eyes and stared out the passenger window at the passing scenery.

"I asked you a question," Marcus said in a stern tone.

Cameron slowly turned to face her man. "Yeah, I'm mad. I'm mad as hell," she said. "You promised that you were done with that shit, and then you turn around and brought it to our son's birthday party? I mean seriously, what the fuck type of shit is that?!"

"First of all, lower your mothafuckin' voice when you talk to me before you wake Justin up."

Cameron turned and looked into the backseat where her son slept peacefully in his car seat. Justin was so adorable with pecan colored skin, the same as his mothers, and short black curly hair. His eyelashes were long and curled upward, and everyone always told her that he looked just like her.

"Second of all," Marcus snapped her back to reality. "I had a lot of shit on my mind—"

Cameron snorted. "Lot of shit like what?" she asked with an attitude.

"Well, for starters, Pandora's Box ain't rakin' in money like it used to," Marcus answered. "As a matter of fact they're talkin' about shuttin' the spot down period altogether—"

"Good," Cameron cut him off. "You said you were done with that dancing shit the same day you promised you were done with the coke—"

"That *dancing shit* paid for your mothafuckin' boutique," Marcus threw up in her face. "That *dancing shit* pays our bills. And *that dancing shit* takes care of our son."

"I'll give you two of those three," Cameron said. "You paid for my boutique and I'll be forever grateful for that, but it's my boutique money that pays the bills and takes care of our son," she argued. "The few lil' dollars you earn now from shaking your dick you're too busy spending on the bullshit you shove up your nose. Maybe once your shit collapses you'll get a fucking clue and snap back to reality."

Marcus turned and looked at Cameron as if she'd just gone crazy. He wasn't used to her speaking to him in such a manner, and it instantly set him off.

Suddenly, in a fit of rage, he yanked his 2013 Cadillac Escalade to the side of the road, and snatched the gears into park.

"Bitch, you must've lost ya mothafuckin' mind talkin' to me like that after all I've done for you. As a matter of fact—the fuck out my damn truck!" he snapped.

Cameron waved Marcus off in a dismissive manner. She was used to his severe mood swings and outbursts. It seemed like the worse his drug addiction got the worst his temper became.

"Marcus, I'm not getting out the damn car," she said. "How else am I going to get home?"

"You think I'm fuckin' playin' don't you?!" He said before opening the driver's door.

Cameron's heart hammered in her chest as she watched him round the truck. They were parked on the side of a busy road. There was no way in hell he was really going to do something crazy. Right? Cameron convinced herself that he wouldn't, but then again she was no stranger to him putting his hands on her.

Marcus yanked open the passenger door, and grabbed Cameron's arm.

"Get the hell off me, Marcus!" Cameron yelled shoving him away.

WHAP!

Marcus slapped the shit out of Cameron before trying to drag her out the passenger seat. She kicked him in a desperate attempt to defend herself, but she was no match against him. He suddenly grabbed her by her shoulder length hair, and brutally yanked her out the car before tossing her to the street like a ragdoll. After slamming the passenger door shut, he rounded the truck and climbed in.

"Marcus!" Cameron quickly jumped to her feet. Tears streamed down her cheeks as she rounded the truck. "Marcus, how the fuck am I going to get home?!"

He ignored Cameron as he slammed the door shut, and sped off.

"*Marcus*!" she screamed.

Stranded and alone, and to make matters worse she had no cellphone to call Ki Ki in order to come pick her up. Her purse and all its belongings were in the passenger seat of Marcus's truck. Cameron felt pathetic as she stood on the side of the road crying. She felt so foolish for staying with a man who treated her three times worse than Silk.

Cameron ran a hand through her wild hair, and looked up and down the busy street. On the opposite side from where she stood was a plaza. She figured maybe someone would be nice enough to lend her their cellphone to call her girl Ki Ki.

Cameron was just about to cross the busy intersection when a silver 2012 Cadillac CTS pulled alongside her. She knew exactly who it was before the driver even lowered the window.

"Cameron, what the hell are you doing out here?" Xavier asked in shock. "Get in."

Cameron quickly rounded the car and climbed into the passenger seat. X's car smelled like a combination of car freshener and marijuana.

Xavier down turned the Wale mixtape he was listening to, and turned on the dome light. Cameron really wished he wouldn't have. As expected, he quickly noticed the reddish bruise on the side of her cheek from where Marcus had slapped her. Xavier decided not to ask any questions as he turned the light off and pulled back into traffic. Cameron had never felt so embarrassed and ashamed in her life.

***

"Yeah, suck on the tip for me," Marcus moaned. He licked his lips in pleasure as his pole was polished with saliva. "Put a lil' bit more spit on it...yeah...like that. Damn girl," he said. "You gon' catch this nut in your mouth?"

Marcus grabbed the base of his dick and slowly massaged it as the mushroom shaped head of his penis was sucked. His toes curled and his thigh muscles tightened as he felt a powerful orgasm approaching.

"Damn...here it comes," he moaned. Seconds later, warm thick not oozed from his dick.

Ki Ki moaned in pleasure as Marcus filled her mouth with his seed. Once she had swallowed all he had to offer, he pulled his flaccid penis from her mouth, and climbed out of his bed.

Ki Ki smiled as she stared at Marcus's tight ass as he made his way to the master bathroom. She and Marcus had been messing around behind Cameron's back for almost six months, and Ki Ki wasn't planning on ending it anytime soon.

Cameron was her best friend, but Ki Ki was enamored with Marcus and had been ever since she first laid eyes on him. He was tall, dark, handsome, and had the bad boy demeanor that she admired. Not to mention he had the best dick game she had ever experienced in her twenty-six years of living.

Ki Ki was slowly but surely falling in love with her best friend's man, and she was to the point where she didn't give a damn about Cameron finding out.

Marcus slowly made his way back inside the bedroom. Beads of perspiration lined his forehead. His girl Cameron had no idea that most times when she went to work he was smashing out her best friend. Unlike, Ki Ki, their secret affair was for intimate purposes only. Ki Ki was a freak, and she sucked a mean dick, but there wasn't a woman in the world that could compete with Cameron for his heart. As fucked up as he treated her at times, he loved her unconditionally.

"Marcus, I have to talk to you," Ki Ki said.

He sighed and took a seat on the edge of the bed. "About what?" he asked nonchalantly.

"About us," Ki Ki smiled. "I'm tired of us having to fuck around on the low."

"Ki Ki, you knew what this shit was when we first started so don't go there with me," Marcus said coolly.

"Well, I didn't think I would fall in love when we first started either," Ki Ki argued.

Marcus snorted. "Bitch, yo' ass ain't in love. Shut that shit up," he said casually.

Ki Ki sucked her teeth and folded her arms. "Marcus, I'm serious," she whined like a toddler who couldn't get their way. "When are you going to leave Cameron—"

"I told yo' simpleminded ass this shit before," Marcus barked. "I'm not leavin' my girl or my mothafuckin' son for nobody!"

"That's not even your damn son!" Ki Ki yelled.

20

Marcus suddenly reached over and slapped the shit out of Ki Ki. The force of the blow was so powerful that she fell off the bed, and landed onto the cream carpeted floor with a thud. Marcus stood to his feet and slowly made his way over towards Ki Ki. His fists were clenched and he looked absolutely enraged by her statement.

"Bitch, don't ever say that shit to me again," he spat.

Ki Ki touched her cheek which stung from the fierce smack. She looked up into Marcus's eyes, and he wasn't at all surprised when her full lips pulled into a sexy smirk.

Marcus scoffed. "I forgot," he said. "You like that shit, huh?"

Ki Ki slowly stood to her feet and walked over towards him. "I'm sorry daddy," she apologized. "I won't say it again. I promise."

Marcus pulled Ki Ki close and kissed her sloppily in the mouth. The two were alike in more ways than one.

***

Cameron pulled her truck up to pump two, and killed the engine. She had just gotten off work an hour ago, and from there she had picked up her son up from daycare. Same routine, different day, but Cameron wouldn't trade it for the world.

"Ka-nee!" Justin cried from the backseat. He may have only been a baby, but he was smart enough to know that candy was sold inside of the gas station.

"Alright, give me a minute to take my seat belt off, son," Cameron laughed.

***

Jude slowly pulled his car up to pump four. The 2001 Ford Taurus vibrated whenever it was turned on, and was tad bit noisy, but he was given the car for free so beggars couldn't be choosers.

Jude had only been out of prison two weeks. He wasn't living the once carefree life that he had grown accustomed to. However, anything was better than being locked up. He had served six months in the Cuyahoga Department Correctional Facility before he was transferred to a minimum security prison. He served six months there and was released for good behavior, but placed on probationary status for a total of thirty-six months, and had to serve an additional six months in a halfway house before he was finally released into the actual community.

Jude was grateful to take whatever he could get. Life, however, wasn't the same as it was before he had gotten locked up, but all he could do was adjust. His condo had been foreclosed, and he now resided in a decent, less than luxurious apartment in Cleveland Heights. Instead of earning the big money he was used to making, he now worked at a factory through a temp agency.

Luckily, Stone had continued to look out for him like he promised, and the moment he was released Stone had his boys hook Jude up with a little cash, a car, and an apartment hookup until he was able to get back on his feet. The task wouldn't be an easy one, but he was determined to get back straight.

Jude turned off the car, climbed out, and made his way towards the gas station to pay for his gas. The moment he opened the door, and stepped inside, he literally froze in place. His heart felt like it had dropped to the pit of his stomach. For a minute, Jude wondered if his eyes were playing tricks on him.

Standing several feet away in line stood Cameron looking just as sexy as she did the night he had met her at the Playpen. She had put on a little weight, but it was in all the right places. She wore a tight fitting black tank top and a pair of Union leggings with studded combat boots.

Cameron was rummaging in her purse for her credit card, and didn't even notice Jude staring at her from afar. His eyes then wandered towards the infant holding onto her leg. Jude's stomach flip-flopped and questions quickly flooded his mind.

How old is he?

Is he mine?

"Excuse me," a female spoke up as she stepped around Jude who stood in the doorway like an idiot.

Cameron looked up, but Jude quickly walked off into a nearby aisle before she was able to see him. He felt so foolish, but he didn't even know what to say her. It had been a year and a half since he had last spoken to her or even laid eyes on her. Jude imagined that she was probably upset with him for pushing her away, but she couldn't even begin to understand the shit he was going through at the time.

Like a fool, he watched from a distance as she paid for her gas, purchased a Blow Pop for the little boy, and exited the store.

Say something, Jude told himself.

What if that baby's not even mine?

What if she's got a dude?

Jude quickly pushed those questions to the back of his mind, paid for his gas, and briskly made his way back to his car. Cameron didn't even notice him walk past as she pumped her gas since she was so busy texting on her phone.

Jude's gaze never left her. Apart of him just wanted to say fuck it, and walk over to her and hold her. He then wanted to tell her how much he loved her, and how sorry he was.

What if she's not even trying to hear that shit, he scolded himself.

The nozzle clicked signaling that the gas was done pumping, and Jude quickly replaced it before climbing into his car. He watched Cameron from his car until she finally finished pumping her gas, and then climbed into her truck. When she pulled off, so did he.

Man, what are you doing, Jude asked himself as he suddenly found himself following Cameron.

***

Xavier lifted his fist to knock on Marcus's front door, but the door suddenly swung open before his fist even connected. Ki Ki had a half smirk on her face as she slowly stepped around Xavier.

"Excuse me," she mumbled before walking towards her car.

Marcus looked shocked to see Xavier standing on the opposite side of his door. "Wassup man? Whatchu' doin' here?" he asked.

"Is it cool if I come in?" Xavier asked. "I wanted to holla at you about somethin'."

Marcus stepped to the side, and allowed Xavier entrance. After closing and locking the door, he padded barefoot to the living room. Xavier followed suit.

Marcus took a seat on his sofa. On the glass coffee table in front of him was a small portion of cocaine. He then used a razor to neatly line it up. Marcus did the shit as if he was in the comforts of his own privacy, and it really bothered Xavier.

"Man, I came over here to talk to you," Xavier said. "I don't wanna see you do that shit."

Marcus looked offended. "Last I checked, nigga, this was my mothafuckin' house," he retorted. With that said he bent down and snorted the line of cocaine. Marcus shivered dramatically, and wiped his nose of any residue.

"Nigga, this the shit I wanted to talk to yo' ass about!" Xavier said. "Nigga, you killin' yo' mothafuckin' self!"

Marcus sucked his teeth and waved his homeboy off. "Nigga, gon' with that shit," he said dismissively. "You wasn't sayin' that when we were poppin' pills and shit."

"Yeah, but you didn't have a family then," Xavier said. "What type of example are you setting for your son, man? And what type of man are you teaching him to be when you throwin' ya girl out the car out in the middle of nowhere?" Xavier shook his head in disappointment. "I'm standin' here talkin' to you, but it feel like I don't even know yo' ass, nigga? The fuck happened to you?"

"You know what happened," Marcus said with a knowing expression.

Xavier shook his head vehemently. "Nah, man. Don't try to put your problems on me—"

"I'm just bein' real. I didn't start shovin' this shit up my nose 'til you get shot—"

"Marcus, grow the fuck up," Xavier said in a disgusted voice. "I used to respect ya ass, but now you just a sorry ass nigga—"

"What?!" Marcus snapped. "The fuck you say?"

"You heard me," Xavier said. "You's a sorry mothafuckin' nigga—"

Marcus suddenly leapt up from the sofa, and ran full speed towards Xavier where he tackled him senselessly. The two hit the hardwood floors with a thud, and proceeded to tussle and wrestle in an attempt to overpower the other.

"Get the fuck off me, man!" Xavier said through gritted teeth.

"Hey! Hey! Hey! What the hell is going on?!" Cameron yelled stepping into the house. Justin was toted up on her hip and even he looked just as clueless as she did.

Both men quickly stood to their feet, and straightened their clothes. Xavier walked towards the front door. He looked pissed the hell off about the entire ordeal. Once he reached the door, he took one look at Cameron then at Marcus and shook his head.

"I don't see how you can deal with this dirty mothafucka," Xavier said before leaving and slamming the front door behind himself.

***

Jude lay awake in bed that evening. He couldn't sleep. All he constantly thought about was Cameron. Unbeknownst to her, he had followed her all that evening all the way up until she finally made it home.

Why didn't you just say something, he asked himself. It had been over a year since Jude had last spoken to her, and he doubted Cameron even felt the same about him. Who was he to burst into her life, and demand that they pick up where they left off? Would she even take him serious? He sure as hell wouldn't.

Jude then turned over onto his side and stared off into the darkness. He thought back to the little boy he saw her with. He looked just like Cameron, but he wondered if the boy was his. The last time Jude and Cameron had spoken to one another she was hollering some abortion shit. At the time, he wasn't trying to hear it, but now he wondered if she had actually gone through with it. He couldn't wait to get his questions answered because if he didn't, the mystery would only eat away at his sanity.

21

Ki Ki giggled as Marcus seductively licked off the small amount of coke that he had placed on her round ass cheek. With his free hand, he slapped her other ass cheek and gave it a firm jiggle.

"Ouch baby," Ki Ki laughed. She then turned over in his bed, and spread her thighs wide open. "I want you to lick some off my pussy now," she said eagerly.

Marcus frowned, and sat up in bed, before swinging his feet around the edge. He wasn't in much of a mood to play anymore. His moods were so up and down. One minute he was hot, the next he was cold.

"What's wrong?" Ki Ki asked sitting up in bed on her knees. She then positioned herself behind Marcus and proceeded to rub his tense shoulders.

"I just can't believe that nigga, Xavier came over here yesterday on that bullshit," he complained. It had happened yesterday, but the shit was still fresh on his mind.

Ki Ki shook her head. "You don't need him anyway," she instigated. "I really wish we could just like...up and leave...go far away. Me and you together. No Xavier. No Justin. No Cameron—"

Marcus instantly flung Ki Ki's hand off him. Evidently, he was not too fond of the fairytale-like ending she had planned for the two of them.

"Yo, how the fuck we start talkin' about me, and then you somehow make the conversation about you?" Marcus asked in a nasty tone.

"I'm sorry," Ki Ki apologized. "I was just saying...I mean...don't you ever get the urge to wanna just up and leave and never look back? Leave your whole life behind," she said. "You never felt like that?"

Marcus looked at Ki Ki like she was crazy. In all actuality, she was. "No," he spat. "Who does that shit?" He then scrutinized Ki Ki through squinted eyes. "And why ya ass even move up here from Georgia? Who the fuck moves to Ohio?" he asked in a sarcastic tone.

Ki Ki remained silent. She wouldn't dare tell him that she had killed the father of her oldest child and fled out of fear. After all, no one knew she had any kids. She had pretty much discarded any and everything that had to do with them including pictures, clothes, and toys. Her mother still had custody of both Tiana and RJ Jr., and Ki Ki had no intentions of regaining custody. They could stay their asses in Georgia for all she cared. She didn't even want to look at them because all she'd see was RJ's stupid face, and then flashbacks of him shoving his bare dick up another man's asshole would come to mind.

Just thinking about RJ, and the level of betrayal he inflicted on Ki Ki set her off. Without thinking clearly, she suddenly slapped Marcus in the face.

He was both surprised and stunned by her reaction. "Are you fuckin' crazy?!" he yelled before punching her in the cheek with a closed fist.

Ki Ki flew backwards and flopped onto the bed before grabbing her sore cheek. Marcus licked away the blood from his bottom lip. He quickly stood to his feet, and walked into his master bathroom.

"I cannot believe you just fuckin' hit me," Marcus said in disbelief. "You really losin' ya fuckin' mind, Ki Ki," he told her.

Marcus had long discovered that Ki Ki had some mental "issues". He dismissed the fact however because he loved to dig her back out, and she showed him a lot more respect than Cameron ever did, but now she had gone a little too far putting her hands on him.

Marcus looked into his reflection in the bathroom mirror at the small cut on his bottom lip. "Aye Ki Ki, if ya ass still in my house by the time I get out this bathroom, we gon' have a mothafuckin' problem..."

"Bay, I'm sorry," Ki Ki cried. "I wasn't thinking—"

"Yeah. You weren't," Marcus agreed. "Get ya shit and get ya ass out my house."

"But Cameron doesn't get off work 'til two," Ki Ki argued. "We still have a couple hours together—"

"Ki Ki, ya ass got ten seconds!" he barked.

Ki Ki took her time getting dressed, and once she was fully clothed she took a seat on the edge of Marcus's bed. Obviously, she was totally unfazed by his threat.

Marcus re-emerged, and saw that Ki Ki hadn't taken heed to his warning. If looks could kill, he would've murdered Ki Ki a dozen times over. "You think I'm fuckin' playin'?" he asked.

Ki Ki smirked. Evidently, she found him to be amusing.

Marcus stomped over towards Ki Ki, snatched her up by her long hair, and literally dragged her out the bedroom. Her crazy ass was actually smiling and giggling the entire time he dragged her to the front door.

After snatching the front door open, he tossed Ki Ki out onto her ass. She slowly picked herself up, and dusted off the fitted spiked shoulder dress she wore.

"You just gonna throw me out?" Ki Ki asked. There was still a look of humor in her expression. "You done got me all horny now...," she smiled.

Marcus wasn't trying to hear that shit as he slammed the door in her face.

***

Jude sat in his Taurus as he patiently waited for Cameron to exit the daycare. He felt like a mini-stalker following her all around the town, but he had finally gathered up enough courage to say something. Now the only thing he worried about was her reaction.

Jude sat in the driver's seat freaking a Black & Mild as he waited. Suddenly, through the rearview mirror, he saw Cameron walk out of the day care and stroll across the parking lot while holding her son's hand. Butterflies quickly formed in his stomach and for a moment, he actually considered driving off.

Taking a deep breath, Jude slowly opened his driver's door and approached her. "Cameron," he called out

Her head quickly whipped in his direction, and she did a double take to be sure her eyes weren't playing tricks on her. Cameron looked like she had just a saw a ghost. Standing several feet from where she stood was the man who had effortlessly stolen her heart from Silk.

Jude wore a fitted black V-neck t-shirt that hugged his toned torso. A pair of dark denim Levis hung off his waist, and an OBEY hat was positioned on his head. His dreads were down instead of tied back like he usually wore them.

"Jude?" Cameron asked in disbelief. "I...thought...I—you..." she stuttered clearly confused and caught off guard.

"They released me early," Jude explained.

"How did you know I would be here?" Cameron asked.

Jude exhaled deeply. "I followed you," he wasn't proud to admit it.

Cameron's mouth closed and opened several times. She didn't know what to say. She still couldn't believe that she was looking at Jude in the flesh. It felt so surreal.

Jude's eyes then wandered down to the little boy holding Cameron's hand. "Is he mine, Cameron?" he asked in a low tone.

Cameron's jaw muscle tensed. She didn't respond immediately as she picked Justin up and placed him on her hip. "No," she finally said. "He's not your son..."

Jude felt a combination of disappointment and anger. His stomach churned as he allowed Cameron's words to sink in. It hurt like hell to hear her say that. His cheeks flushed as he stared intensely at his ex-girlfriend. "So you aborted my baby...?" Jude's voice cracked as he spoke. "You killed my kid and had some other nigga's baby? That's what you're telling me...?"

"You gotta lot of nerve even showing up here," Cameron said in a nasty tone. "If memory serves me correctly you turned your damn back on me," she reminded him. "It wasn't the other way around. I wrote you constantly, I came up to visit you...I tried to show you where my loyalty was...but you showed me you didn't want that," she said. "I'm only human...and I had to learn to move on...without you," she added.

"Cameron...I...I fucked up by pushing you away," Jude admitted. "My intentions were never to hurt you—"

"But you did," Cameron cut him off. "And then you had the nerve to send me those bullshit ass Pre-paid cards," she spat. "I didn't need your damn money, Jude...I needed you."

"I needed you too," Jude said. "I still do..."

Cameron shook her head. “It’s too late for that now...”

Jude didn’t like the way that sounded. “I don’t know what kind of impression you got from me sending that money to you, but it wasn’t like that,” he explained. “I wanted you to know that I cared...but I just didn’t know how to say it,” Jude admitted. “Cameron, I was going through a lot.”

“And I wasn’t?” Cameron asked.

Jude nodded in agreement. “I fucked up...I’m sorry.”

There was an uncomfortable silence between the two.

“Can I ask what did you do with the money I sent you?” Jude asked.

Cameron shifted Justin from her left hip to her right. She stared into Jude’s dark eyes. As pissed as she was with him, she would be lying to herself if she said she didn’t love him.

“I put the money in our son’s account,” she told him. Marcus had no idea that she had even opened up a bank account for Justin, and she didn’t think he needed to know. Cameron had to do the right thing by investing in her son’s future, and she couldn’t risk Marcus wasting the money on his drug addiction.

Jude stood in silence for several seconds. A smile slowly crept across his face. He was relieved to hear that. “So this is my son...”

Cameron grimaced. Initially, it wasn't in her intentions to tell Jude, but the fact of the matter was, he deserved to know. She couldn't deprive him of that. She nodded her head.

Jude paused. "Can I hold him?" he asked timidly.

"I don't think that's a good idea," Cameron quickly responded.

Jude looked disappointed. "But this is my son, Cameron..."

Cameron mulled over the decision for a second, and then slowly made her way towards Jude. She handed him Justin and a wide grin spread across Jude's face as he took his son from her.

"Hey man," Jude said.

Justin began playing with one of Jude's dreads.

"Hey, man. You know who I am?" Jude asked him. "What his name?" he asked Cameron.

She folded her arms underneath her breasts. "Justin," she answered.

Justin was so preoccupied with toying with Jude's dreadlocks that nothing else mattered to him. Jude kissed his son's forehead and hugged him tightly. Tears formed in his eyes as he held on to his child for the first time.

Jude then looked over at Cameron. "Thank you," he said. He was so relieved and happy to know that she hadn't gone through with the abortion. Jude then held his hand out for Cameron signaling for her to come closer.

She stared at his outstretched hand for several seconds before finally unfolding her arms, and walking over towards him. Without a word, Cameron placed her hand in Jude's and he slowly pulled her into his embrace.

Holding onto Cameron and Justin, Jude never wanted to let them ago as they stood in the parking lot of Justin's daycare. The tender moment was suddenly interrupted when Cameron's cellphone rang.

Cameron quickly pulled away from Jude in order to see who was calling. To her dismay, it was Marcus. "I've gotta go," she said.

"Who is that? Yo' nigga?" Jude wanted to know.

Cameron took Justin from him. "I'm sorry, Jude..." She quickly headed towards her car.

Jude followed after Cameron. There was a look of disappointment on his face. "I don't wanna live my life without you and my son in it, Cameron..."

Cameron placed Justin inside of his car seat, closed the back door, and turned to face Jude. "I'm sorry...but I'm with someone else now—"

"Leave that nigga," Jude said.

Cameron sighed in frustration. "It's not that easy, Jude," she explained. "Marcus has been there for me. He's helped raise our son. I can't just rip that away from him."

Jude nodded his head in understanding. "I can respect that," he said. "But can I ask you something, Cameron," he began. "Are you happy?"

Cameron turned on her heel, and headed to the driver's side of the truck. "Good bye, Jude," she said.

"You can't answer the question?" Jude asked.

Cameron climbed inside her truck, and slammed the door closed. Jude watched as she navigated out of the parking lot.

"Damn..."

22

Cameron watched as Marcus gathered a few of his dancing outfits and props, and tossed them into his black duffel bag. He was on his way to do a bachelorette party for some random soon-to-be-wife. Cameron wasn't digging it at all. There was no telling what all Marcus would do behind closed doors just to earn some quick and convenient cash. However, she couldn't sweat him about it too hard because she knew what his profession entailed before she even became romantically involved with him.

"What time is the party going to be over?" Cameron asked standing in the doorway of their bedroom.

"I'm not sure. Could last an hour, could last a few hours," Marcus answered nonchalantly.

Cameron sighed and ran a hand through her brown shoulder length hair. "Marcus...you know you don't have to do this shit anymore. I could help you try to find a job somewhere. Maybe you could take some classes—"

"Cameron, stop tryin' to turn me into one of those white collar type of niggas. The fact that I'm gettin' money should be enough for you to lay off," he snapped. "Doesn't matter what I'm doin' to get it as long as it's legal. Damn, you can be such a fuckin' headache..."

Cameron folded her arms beneath her breasts. "I'm a headache because I want what's best for you?"

"Nah. You want what's best for ya damn self," Marcus retorted. "I wonder did you give ya boy, Silk a hard ass time about him strippin'?" he asked. "Shit, 'cuz if memory serves me right, I could've sworn ya ass was all up in the shows, cheesin' and recordin' his ass like you were so fuckin' proud."

Cameron scoffed and shook her head in disbelief. "I was younger then," she admitted. "I thought differently than I do now. Hell, you don't see me climbing on the pole," she said. "I'm not about that life anymore."

Marcus zipped up his duffel bag. "Well, I am," he said flatly. He pulled the duffel bag strap over his shoulder and walked over towards Cameron.

Marcus then leaned down in order to place a kiss on her lips, but she quickly turned her head away.

He immediately understood what her cool gesture meant. However, he was not about to kiss her ass. "Lock the door behind me," he said.

Cameron followed behind Marcus as he made his way to the front door. He unlocked the door, but before he opened it, he turned around to face Cameron.

"You need to stop tryin' to change a nigga, and just accept me for me," Marcus said. "I'm not perfect...but I damn sure wasn't when you met me." With that said, he opened the front door and walked out.

***

Jude knew he was behaving impulsively as he eased his car into the cul de sac where Cameron resided. Then again, he had no other way of getting in contact with her. He wouldn't be able to sleep peacefully if he didn't get another opportunity to talk to her that day. When Jude had seen Cameron earlier, there were so many thoughts running through his mind, and so many emotions he were experiencing, that he wasn't able to convey how he truly felt.

Aside from that, Jude couldn't sit back and accept the fact that Cameron was allowing some nigga to raise his son. Shit was different when he was behind bars. There wasn't much he could do for her then—or for himself for that matter. Cameron and Jude had history, and now that he was out he was ready to rekindle what they once had. Damn whatever dude she was booed up with now. His ass was irrelevant in Jude's eyes.

Cameron had told Jude that her love and loyalty would forever remain with him, but he wondered if she truly meant that. He was prepared to put her statement to the ultimate test.

Jude killed the engine to his car, but before he could even step out he watched as Cameron's front door opened. Marcus walked out with a duffel bag hanging off his shoulder, and headed towards his truck.

Jude sucked his teeth. "This nigga," he mumbled. He recognized Marcus immediately, and it took everything in him not to jump out of his car, run over towards him, and steal own his ass while he least expected it.

Marcus opened the back door of his Cadillac Escalade, tossed the duffel bag into the backseat, and climbed inside the truck. Jude watched as Marcus slowly backed out of his driveway and pulled off.

Jude shook his head. "Nigga, I hope you kissed ya girl goodbye," he said to himself.

***

Cameron had just put Justin to sleep, and was about to take a hot shower when there was a knock at her front door. Marcus had left no less than three minutes ago, but she assumed maybe he had forgotten something and come back.

Cameron padded barefoot to the front door, and peered through the peephole. Her breath instantly caught in her chest! She quickly opened the front door. "Jude—how—what—how did you—"

Cameron's words were immediately cut off after Jude gently grabbed her by the face, and eagerly crushed his lips against hers. With everything that Cameron had said earlier in the parking lot, Jude was surprised that she didn't even fight his kiss in the slightest. She immediately gave in to him, and it was then that he knew she felt the exact same way about him as he felt about her.

Jude stepped inside Cameron's home, and kicked the door closed with his foot. Not once did they break their kiss. Cameron wrapped her arms around Jude's neck as they indulged a wild, passionate kissing session. In the midst of their rampant kissing and groping, Jude backed Cameron against the foyer accent table. The table shook slightly, and a framed picture of Cameron and Marcus fell onto the hardwood floor before shattering.

Neither Jude nor Cameron seemed to notice or care. Jude lifted Cameron's right leg up, and gave her ass a mannish squeeze. He was usually never that aggressive, but nearly two years without any pussy had him behaving barbarically.

"Wait...wait..." Cameron whispered pulling away from Jude.

"What's wrong?" Jude asked with a concerned expression.

"We shouldn't be doing this," she said. "You know I'm with someone..."

Jude stared into Cameron's eyes unblinkingly. "Look me in the eyes, and tell me you don't want this, and then I'll leave," he said. "But I can't promise I won't come back," he smiled.

Cameron bit her bottom lip seductively, before pressing her lips against his. Jude quickly picked her up bridal style, and headed in the direction of where he thought her bedroom was.

"No, that's the baby's bedroom," Cameron giggled.

Jude entered the bedroom on the opposite side of the hallway which was actually a guest bedroom. He carefully lay down on the queen size bed. They hurriedly undressed simultaneously, and before they were able to think twice about their actions or the possible consequences they were rolling around in the sheets.

Jude positioned himself in between Cameron's thighs. He then lifted her left leg over his shoulder, and slid deep inside her wetness.

"*Oooh*," Cameron whimpered. "Jude...*damn*..."

Jude pushed his dreads out his way so that he could see Cameron's beautiful sex expressions as he sped up his pace.

"*Mmmm*," Cameron moaned. "Slow down a little...," she begged.

Jude wasn't trying to hear that. He purposely wanted to beat her pussy up to the point where she would be too sore to have sex with Marcus.

Jude flipped Cameron over onto her stomach, and lifted her round ass up, and slowly slipped inside of her. The sound of the wetness between her thighs was music to his ears.

Jude quickly sped his pace up, and grabbed onto Cameron's shoulders as his pelvis slapped against her ass. Cameron held onto the headboard for support as Jude pounded into her. She bit her bottom lip to keep from screaming, and waking up their son.

Jude bent down and trailed his tongue along Cameron's back. He then worked his way towards her neck before nibbling on her earlobe. He reached his hand underneath her and fondled her moist clit.

"You still love me?" Jude whispered in Cameron's ear. His rapid pace quickly turned into slow, even strokes.

"Yes! Yes!" Cameron cried out.

Jude smiled confidently. "Good. That's all I need to know," he said.

He pulled out of Cameron and rolled over onto his back before positioning her on top of him. She slid down onto his pole and bounced up and down.

Jude palmed her round breasts. "Fuck me like you love me, Cam," he moaned.

"*Oooohh,*" Cameron whimpered. "I'm about to cum!"

Jude grabbed Cameron's waist, and thrust his hips forward. Seconds later, they came together simultaneously. Cameron dropped limply onto the bed beside Jude. They panted and attempted to regain their normal breathing.

"You know I'm not gon' let this nigga have you, right?" Jude asked Cameron as he stared up at the ceiling.

Cameron turned onto her side, propped her elbow up, and rested her head on her hand. "We would've never been in this predicament if you hadn't pushed me away," she said in a low tone.

"I know baby," Jude agreed. "I know you may have thought I was just bein' selfish, but I wasn't. It's about you…it's always been about you. But after Jerrell died I just couldn't think straight—"

"Jerrell died?" Cameron asked in disbelief. "I'm sorry…I had no idea…" Suddenly, Jude's actions were beginning to make sense. "I'm really sorry to hear that…" It was because of Jerrell that Jude and Cameron even met in the first place.

Jude turned to face Cameron and stared into her eyes. "Tell me what I gotta do to make us a family," he said.

Cameron leaned closer to Jude and planted a soft kiss on his lips. "You can start by never pushing me away again," she said. "I'm always going to be there for you." She reached over and ran her fingers through his dreadlocks. "You know that."

Jude took Cameron's hand and placed a gentle kiss on the back it. "I know that now babe," he said. "I'ma always be there for you too," he promised. "I'm not the same nigga you met a couple years ago with all that money and stuntin' and shit, but I still have the same heart. And I still feel the same way about you now as I felt then."

Cameron smiled. "The money doesn't matter to me. You'll always be the same guy that I fell in love with. The same guy who was giving me a hard time over a lap dance," she laughed.

Jude chuckled as he reflected back to the night he met Cameron.

"You'd better go before Marcus gets back," she said.

Jude scoffed. “I want that nigga to come back,” he said in a confrontational tone. “That way I can beat his ass and steal you from him.”

Cameron smirked and shook her head.

Jude leaned over and kissed Cameron on the forehead. “Think about what I said, aight?”

Cameron nodded her head.

“I’m waitin’ on you to hopefully make the right choice,” Jude said.

23

The following afternoon Ki Ki and Cameron strolled through Aurora Farms Outlet to do some much-needed shopping while having a little girl time. Initially, Cameron decided against telling a soul about Jude returning into her life, but she needed to talk to someone about it and hopefully get some advice about the situation.

"So what are you going to do about Marcus?" Ki Ki asked as they walked past the Tommy Hilfiger store.

"I don't know," Cameron answered. "I really don't know."

"You sound like you pretty much got your mind made up about who you want to be with," Ki Ki noted.

Cameron looked over at Ki Ki. "I do have my mind made up," she admitted. "But then there's a part of me that feels like I'm obligated to Marcus. Like I owe him for everything's he done for me," she said. "When I first met him I was struggling with school, and with paying the mortgage on the house, and on top of that I was pregnant." Cameron shook her head. "There's not a lot of guys who would've done what Marcus did for me. He supported me all throughout my pregnancy, and as you can see, he treats Justin like he's his own flesh and blood."

"Yeah, but you told me Jude's done a lot for you too," Ki Ki argued. "Honestly, if I were you, I'd say fuck Marcus and go back to Jude." Ki Ki was only saying that because she wanted Cameron out of the picture so she could have Marcus all to herself. Cameron's actual happiness was the last thing she cared about.

Cameron mulled over the decision. "It's like...when I first saw Jude...all those old emotions came back." She shook her head. "The crazy thing is...I don't think I ever stopped loving Jude. And as fucked up as this sounds...I don't think I ever loved Marcus..."

Ungrateful bitch, Ki Ki thought to herself. "You just gotta do what makes you happy, Cameron," she forced out. "You just gotta do what makes you happy."

***

The moment Cameron went off for a quick bathroom break, Ki Ki slipped inside of the Nike outlet, pulled out her cellphone, and called Marcus.

He answered on the fourth ring. "What do want, Ki Ki?" Marcus asked in an irritated tone. Obviously, he was still upset about their last time spent together.

"You still mad at me, bay?" Ki Ki purred into the phone.

"Bitch, you slapped me in the mothafuckin' face. What do you think?" Marcus asked sarcastically.

"I told you I was just trippin'. I must be 'bout to start my period," Ki Ki said matter-of-factly.

"What do you want Ki Ki?" Marcus asked again. "I'm doin' somethin' right now..."

"When are we going to get to spend time with each other again?" she asked. "I miss the way your cum tastes," she whispered.

Usually her dirty talk would have gotten Marcus aroused, but this time around it had the opposite effect. "Look, I'm really startin' to be cool on yo' ass," he said. "You just be doin' a lil' too much for me."

"What are you saying?" Ki Ki asked knowing damn well what Marcus meant.

"I don't wanna fuck with yo' ass no mo'," Marcus said coolly. "Ya ass need to get some mental help, 'cuz it's obvious you got a world of issues."

Ki Ki's cheeks flushed in anger. If she was standing anywhere near Marcus she would have slit his jugular. "We've been fucking with each other for six months and now all of a sudden you wanna end it—"

"End it?!" Marcus repeated. "Bitch, it wasn't never shit from the jump other than me gettin' some pussy and you gettin' some dick."

Tears pooled in Ki Ki's eyes. "But I love you..."

CLICK.

Ki Ki pulled the cellphone away from her face, and stared at in disbelief. Feeling like she had something to prove, she immediately called Marcus back.

He answered on the second ring. "What?!" he snapped.

"You better take back that shit you said," Ki Ki threatened.

"And if I don't, what your fat ass gon' do?"

Ki Ki's face became hotter by the second. Just hearing him call her 'fat' made her think of RJ. She then thought about his fate and a smile slowly crept across her lips. "You're right," Ki Ki said. "You don't have to be worried about me. Because if I were you I'd be more concerned about the nigga that just got out of prison whose trying to take his woman and child away from your coke head ass."

Marcus was silent for a brief period. "The fuck is yo' crazy ass talking about?" he asked.

"You know exactly who I'm talking about," Ki Ki said. "Or if you don't believe me, why don't you go look at the sheets in your guest bedroom. You might be able to see some cum stains from when Cameron got fu—"

CLICK.

A wide grin spread across Ki Ki's face. She didn't bother calling back Marcus that time. Her point had been proven.

***

Marcus walked up behind Cameron, and kissed the side of her neck as she stirred around the pot of spaghetti. "I really love you baby," he confessed.

The hairs on the back of Cameron's neck stood erect. She couldn't even fix her mouth up to return the words of affection.

Marcus slowly made his way over towards the kitchen island and took a seat on one of the barstools. "Cameron, can I ask you a question," he said.

"Of course," Cameron answered with her back turned to him.

"You'd keep it real with me no matter what, right?" Marcus asked.

"Of course," Cameron said.

The shit Ki Ki had told Marcus earlier that day really got to him, but nothing hurt worse than the fact that he knew what she had said was the truth. "So you would tell me anything, right?" he asked Cameron.

"Yes..."

"And when I say anything I mean *anything*...," Marcus stressed.

Cameron paused, and Marcus didn't miss her tense up.

There's no way he could possibly know, she convinced herself. *Ki Ki is the only one who knows about Jude coming over last night and there's no way in hell my girl would tell Marcus.*

"Yes…I'd tell you anything," Cameron said in a low tone as she continued to mix the sauce in with the penne noodles.

Marcus's jaw tensed. It took everything in him not to jump off the barstool and whup Cameron's ass. He was giving her the benefit of the doubt. He wanted to see if she'd be woman enough to at least tell the truth.

"So you'd tell me if your ex got out of prison, and wanted you back in his life?" Marcus asked.

Cameron's heart felt like it had sank into the pit of her stomach. *Maybe he's just asking random questions,* she thought to herself. *He doesn't know shit.*

"Yes…I would tell you," Cameron answered.

Marcus shook his head in disbelief. His fists were clenched, and he was really trying to keep his cool because if he went ham on Cameron he'd probably kill her.

"And you'd tell me if you let that nigga in my house, and fucked him in my bed, right?" Marcus asked.

The wooden spoon dropped from Cameron's hands, and landed onto the kitchen floor. Spaghetti sauce splattered the heated tile floors. Marcus had Cameron shook, and he knew it.

Cameron quickly bent down, retrieved the wooden spoon, and wiped the mess up. "Yes, Marcus," she answered. "But you know I'd never do anything like that."

I could strangle this bitch, Marcus thought to himself. He slowly stood from his seat and made his way over towards Cameron. He softly touched her shoulder, and noticed her instantly tense up from his touch.

"Good. I'm glad to know that," Marcus said. "Because I'd be extremely hurt if you betrayed me."

Cameron turned around to face Marcus. *Just tell him it's over,* she said to herself. *Tell him you don't want to be with him anymore.*

"I wouldn't," Cameron lied.

Fuck me.

Why didn't I tell him?

"I really, really love you and Justin a lot," Marcus said. "And I know we aren't the ideal, perfect family, but I love what we got," he told her. "I'd go crazy if a nigga tried to come into the picture, and break up what we have...As a matter of fact, I'd probably kill him..."

24

Cameron's small boutique was located inside of a plaza in Mayfield Heights. She got pretty decent business there, and she also ran an online boutique for the convenience of people who didn't reside in Ohio. She loved her cute, little boutique which she had named after her aunt Linda who had passed away last year due to congested heart failure.

Cameron was sorting through her latest shipment when Ki Ki strolled inside her boutique with a stupid ass Kool-Aid grin on her face.

"Hey, Cam. What's up, girl?" she greeted cheerfully.

Cameron stepped from behind the counter and folded her arms underneath her breasts. There was a serious expression on her pretty face. "You tell me," she said.

"What's up? What do you mean?" Ki Ki asked dumbfounded.

"Ki Ki, you were the only person I told about Jude. If you weren't my best friend, I wouldn't have told a soul," Cameron said. "Last night, Marcus began making accusations about me cheating on him. He wouldn't have known that on his own."

Ki Ki didn't respond.

"I hate that I'm about to even ask you this question because I shouldn't have to," Cameron continued. "But did you tell Marcus what I told you?"

Ki Ki sighed dejectedly. "No..."

"Ki Ki," Cameron said in a no-nonsense tone. "Be real. We're best friends, right?"

Ki Ki nodded her head.

"Alright, I'm gonna ask you this again," Cameron said. "Did you tell Marcus what I told you yesterday?"

Ki Ki paused and debated whether or not to be honest. "He needed to know..."

Cameron looked mortified and confused at the same time. "He needed to know?!" she repeated. "What the hell are you talking about? And why would you tell *my* man some shit like that Ki Ki? When the fuck did you even have the time to be talking to Marcus?!"

"Why do you even care?" Ki Ki spat. "You said so yourself yesterday that you never loved him! You don't even want him!"

"You telling me this shit like ya'll fucking!" Cameron yelled. "Is that it?! Huh? Ya'll fucking or some shit?!"

Ki Ki's silence said it all.

Cameron looked hurt and disappointed. She shook her head in disbelief. "I can't fucking believe you," she said. Then again Ki Ki wasn't Cameron's first friend to go behind her back and fuck her man. Pocahontas had given her a taste of what that felt like.

"Cameron, I'm sorry, but you should've—"

Cameron didn't even give Ki Ki a chance to finish her sentence as she lunged at her, and grabbed a handful of her hair. In a sudden fit of rage, Cameron began raining blows all over Ki Ki's face and head.

Ki Ki tried her best to defend herself, but she never really was much of a fighter as crazy as her ass was.

Cameron suddenly tossed her into a nearby rack of clothing. Ki Ki crashed into it, and it fell onto the floor. Before she could recuperate, Cameron jumped on top her, hitting and punching every part of Ki Ki's body that she could reach.

Ki Ki shielded her face as she ate Cameron's devastating blows. Once Cameron, had finally tired herself out, she stood to her feet, and backed away.

Ki Ki sat up on the floor, and wiped away the blood trickling from her nose and lip. She then had the nerve to smile revealing her bloodstained teeth. "You done?" she asked. She seemed amused if anything when the average chick would have been crying instead.

"Bitch, get your crazy ass up out my mothafuckin' store," Cameron spat.

Ki Ki picked herself up from the ground, and stumbled towards the exit. "You didn't love him,

Cameron," she said. "Don't be mad because another bitch did..."

"Bitch, I said get the hell out my damn store!" Cameron yelled with clenched fists.

Ki Ki surprised Cameron when she didn't look the least bit fearful about getting her ass whupped again. She did however leave the store without another word.

Cameron looked around her boutique at the fallen rack, and the clothes scattered on the floor. She felt a mixture of betrayal and disappointment.

"What the fuck?!" Cameron yelled in anger.

***

"Stupid fucking bitch!" Ki Ki yelled as she sat inside her car. She was parked outside of Cameron's boutique. "Why did you fucking do that?!" she hollered to no one in particular.

Suddenly, and without warning, Ki Ki punched herself in the face. Her fist was covered with her own blood, but she didn't seem to care as she punched herself several more times.

"Stupid! Stupid! Fucking stupid bitch!" she screamed.

Ki Ki's Camry rocked slightly as she went ham on herself inside her car. By the time she finished assaulting herself her face was a bloodied mess, and she was barely even recognizable.

"They think I'm fucking crazy," she said to herself. "I'ma show their asses crazy..."

***

When Cameron pulled up to her house, she noticed that Marcus was leaving. She was so flustered that she almost forgot to put the truck in park as she hopped out.

"You off work early, babe," Marcus said. "I was actually on my way to the gym," he told her walking towards his truck.

"Really?" Cameron asked skeptically. "Or were you on your way over to Ki Ki's house to fuck?!" she spat.

Marcus looked shocked. He couldn't believe that Cameron finally knew. *Oh, this bitch done went too far*, he thought to himself. The very next time he saw Ki Ki's big-mouth ass he planned on slapping the shit out of her.

"You look surprised," Cameron said nodding her head. "Yeah, I know. I just can't believe you'd do some shit like that to me, and with my best friend of all people!"

Cameron cried the same song in the hospital with Silk when she found out about him sleeping with Pocahontas.

"Cameron, you ain't no fuckin' better," Marcus spat. "So don't stand here and play the fuckin' victim when you fucked that nigga in my house yesterday."

"And you know what? I feel damn good about it now too."

Marcus's nostrils flared in anger. He instantly dropped his gym bag, walked over towards Cameron, and slapped the hell out of her. "I can't believe you would disrespect me!" he yelled. "I should have whupped ya mothafuckin' ass yesterday when you stood in my face and lied. I tried to give ya hoe ass a chance to be honest!"

Suddenly, Cameron spat a mouthful of blood into Marcus's face. "Fuck you!" she yelled. "I'm sick of your ass! I've *been* sick of you and your shit! Your temper! Your drug addiction! Your cheating! I'm done with your ass! You ain't shit but another Silk!"

Marcus wiped the blood out his eye. "Don't ever compare me to that dead ass mothafucka!" he yelled. "He couldn't even take care of his own kid, and yet I'm takin' care of yours, and the lil' nigga ain't even mine!"

"Yeah, thank God he's not," Cameron retorted. "But don't worry. You won't ever have to do shit else for me and mine because it's over!" She tried to walk around Marcus but he quickly jumped in front of her. "Get the hell out my way, and let me get my stuff."

"You go in there and touch that shit, I'ma beat ya mothafuckin' ass all up and down this street," Marcus threatened.

"You're not going to make me stay somewhere I don't want to be," Cameron said. "I'm leaving you, and you'll never see me and my son again—"

Marcus roughly snatched up Cameron by her arm. "You not takin' my mothafuckin' son nowhere!" he yelled.

***

Jude was on one that afternoon as he drove down Cameron's street. He had told her that he'd wait for her to make her mind up, but the fact of the matter was, he couldn't wait at all, and he'd only seen her last two days ago.

Jude needed Cameron by his side everyday three-hundred and sixty-five days a year. He couldn't stand the thought of her being with another man anymore. He was coming to reclaim what was rightfully his, and if her dude wanted to step to him crazy then he was planning on dropping his ass where he stood.

As Jude neared Cameron's home, he noticed her and Marcus standing in the driveway arguing. His face instantly grew hot as he watched Marcus roughly snatch Cameron up her arm. Without deliberation, he parked alongside the curb, yanked the gears into Park, and killed the engine.

"Aye!" Jude barked as he quickly made his way across the street. "Nigga, you better get yo' mothafuckin' hands off my girl!"

Marcus and Cameron turned their attention towards Jude whose fists were clenched tightly as he approached them.

Marcus turned Cameron loose in order to give his undivided attention to Jude. "Your girl?!" he repeated. "Nigga, what ya'll had is dead and gone," he spat. "You might've gotten a lil' pussy yesterday, but your son calls me daddy, nigga!"

Jude was just about to run up on Marcus and steal his ass, but the abrupt sound of tires burning asphalt grabbed all three of their attention.

Ki Ki opened her driver's door, and stepped out. Suddenly, she aimed her 9mm in Marcus, Jude, and Cameron's direction. It was the same gun she had used to kill Tiana's father.

Everything seemingly happened in the blink of an eye! Ki Ki squeezed the trigger several times.

POP!

POP!

POP!

POP!

The first bullet shattered the back window of Marcus's Cadillac Escalade. The second one lodged in the exterior of the truck. The third bullet shattered Marcus's living room window, and the fourth hit Cameron.

25

Cameron immediately fell backwards from the impact of the gunshot. Jude quickly caught her before she hit the concrete.

Ki Ki quickly jumped back inside her car and skirted off.

"*You fuckin'bitch*!" Marcus yelled before he took off running after Ki Ki's car.

Jude slowly lowered himself onto the ground. Blood instantly drenched Cameron's white sleeveless dress shirt. Her eyes were closed, and she was motionless.

"Cameron," Jude croaked out. Tears streamed down his cheeks. "Get some mothafuckin' help!" he screamed.

Marcus was in a world of his own as he continued to chase after Ki Ki's car although it was no use since she was nowhere near the scene.

Jude touched Cameron's cheeks with trembling fingers. "No. No. No. No. No," he cried. "You're going to be okay. It's going to be okay," he said. He stood up and lifted Cameron's limp body into his arms.

Marcus finally returned to the house with a look of anger in his eyes. He was hell-bent on making Ki Ki pay.

"Get some mothafuckin' help man!" Jude cried.

Marcus ignored Jude as he climbed inside his Cadillac Escalade and skirted out of the driveway.

***

Marcus couldn't believe that Ki Ki's simpleminded ass had actually gone straight home after the shit she had pulled. Yet sure enough her Toyota Camry was parked in the driveway in front of her ran down duplex. She hadn't made any type of come up in almost two years.

Marcus pulled his truck crookedly into her driveway, parking halfway on her dilapidated front lawn. After hopping out of his truck, he ran up to the front door. Not bothering to knock on it, he proceeded to viciously kick her front door.

"*Bitch, I know you in there*!" Marcus screamed like a maniac.

Nearby neighbors slowly exited their homes to see what all the commotion was. In that specific neighborhood, they had 911 on speed dial for when shit like this happened. One of the neighbors quickly ran inside their home and dialed the police.

Marcus continued to kick the front door, until he finally kicked the raggedy door off the hinges.

"Bitch, where you at?!" Marcus screamed. "I know you in here!"

He ran through the entire downstairs looking for Ki Ki, but didn't find her. Marcus anxiously raced upstairs towards her bedroom where the door was closed. He pressed his ear against the door, and listened to Ki Ki's muffled cries.

Backing away from the door, Marcus drew his leg back, and viciously kicked the bedroom door open.

Ki Ki sat on her bed crying and holding the gun in her hands. She shook her head vehemently. "I'm sorry, Marcus," she cried. "I didn't mean to do it...I just—I lost it."

Marcus slowly made his way over towards Ki Ki. He looked like a psychopath as he approached her with clenched fists.

"Marcus, please," Ki Ki cried raising her gun towards him. "I love you...I don't wanna shoot you..."

Marcus was not trying to hear that shit as he continued to approach Ki Ki.

With trembling fingers, Ki Ki aimed the gun towards his head, and squeezed the trigger.

POP!

A single bullet flew past Marcus's head, but not before grazing his left ear slightly. Blood trickled from his ear and ran down the side of his neck, but he didn't seem to notice or care.

Ki Ki raised the gun towards him again, preparing to take aim for a second time. Marcus quickly slapped the gun out her hands. It slid over towards her dresser.

Marcus suddenly wrapped his calloused hands around Ki Ki's slender throat, and squeezed with all his strength. One of her eyes shot open in its socket. The other was swollen shut from when she had beaten herself earlier. Ki Ki clawed at his hands, but the more she fought, the harder Marcus squeezed. Images of Cameron's motionless body in Jude's arms came to mind, and all he could think about was making Ki Ki suffer.

Marcus slowly climbed on top of her, and bared his teeth like a mad man as he strangled her to death. Her cheeks quickly turned beet red, and the blood vessels in her eyes burst. After seconds, she stopped moving and trying to fight with him completely.

Ki Ki was dead.

Marcus slowly released the vice grip he had locked around her throat, and stood to his feet. Ki Ki's eyes were wide open as she continued to stare at the ceiling. He was so out of it that he didn't even hear the rapid footsteps racing up the stairs.

"*Get on the ground*!" An officer barked as he aimed his gun at Marcus. Several police officers stood nearby with their weapons aimed and ready to fire if need be.

Marcus slowly turned around to face the police officers. Gradually, he lowered himself onto his knees, and allowed the officers to cuff him. It wasn't until then, that he realized the consequences of his many actions.

26

One Week Later.

Jude knocked on the wooden door before slowly making his way inside. He had his son in his arms, and for the first time in a long time, he actually looked happy regardless of everything he had gone through.

Cameron sat up in the hospital bed. There wasn't an ounce of makeup on her pretty face, but she was still flawless in Jude's eyes.

A wide grin spread across her face at the sight of the two most important men in her life.

"Look who's awake," Jude said.

Cameron held her arms out for her son who had his own little arms outstretched.

Jude carefully handed Justin to Cameron. Her shoulder and chest were bandaged. The bullet had impaled her upper chest before going clean through her back, but luckily no major arteries had been hit.

Jude was relieved to know that Cameron had simply fainted after she had been shot.

He leaned down and kissed the top of Cameron's hair before taking a seat in the visitor's chair beside her bed. "How are you feeling, bay?" he asked in a concerned tone.

"Ready to get back to my life," Cameron smiled.

It was ironic how almost two years ago, she hated her life. With all the drama, fighting, and betrayal she had put up with she wondered if her life would ever change for the good and luckily it did starting with Jude.

The day she had gone to the abortion clinic she barely made it to the front door before she quickly turned around and hopped back inside her truck. That was the best decision she had ever made in her life. Cameron also ended up running into Silk's sister Tamika a few months into her pregnancy, and offered a heartfelt apology about Silk's death. She was relieved when Tamika accepted her apology, and even showed up to Cameron's baby shower bearing gifts.

If Cameron would have run into Pure Seduction she would have offered the same heartfelt outfit apology, but the last she heard of Pure Seduction was that she had gotten her grill fixed, and ran off with some pimp to Miami. Cameron was just relieved to be rid of the drama so she could finally lead a peaceful life.

Cameron, however, was disheartened about Marcus's fate. He had gotten twenty years for Ki Ki's brutal murder.

"You won't have to be in here for too much longer," Jude said snapping Cameron from her thoughts.

She smiled. "Thank God," she said. "It's boring in here. I miss my boys."

Cameron bounced her son up and down on her knee, and played with him. Jude sat back and watched in silence enjoying the sight of his family.

"Cameron, I have to tell you something," Jude finally said.

She turned to face him. "What's that?" she asked.

Jude took a deep breath. "I don't ever wanna lose you again," he admitted. "I know we been through a lot of shit these past these few years, and I'm man enough to admit that I fucked up. A lot of it was my fault. I shouldn't have been pushin' you away when we supposed to be each other's rock," he explained. "And I promise you that that shit won't happen again. I lost you once, and I'm not gonna lose you again...I wanna make this shit official. I wanna marry you...make you Mrs. Jude Patterson. And a nigga ain't got the money right now to buy you the biggest rock I can afford, but once I get on my feet, I promise you got that."

Cameron scoffed and shook her head. "I don't care about the biggest rock," she told him. "I don't care about the money. I don't want any of that," she said. "I just want you..."

PART 4 IS AVAILABLE NOW! CLICK HERE TO GET YOUR COPY!

MORE **GREAT** BOOKS CONNECTED TO THE **CAMERON** SERIES!!!

JADED PUBLICATIONS Presents

Wife Of A

MISFIT

JADE JONES

JADED PUBLICATIONS Presents
SOUL
&
Diana
AN ATLANTA LOVE STORY
JADE JONES

JADED PUBLICATIONS Presents
Uncovered
SECRETS
JADE JONES

JADED PUBLICATIONS Presents
Gambino
&
POCAHONTAS
A Ghetto Love Story
JADE JONES

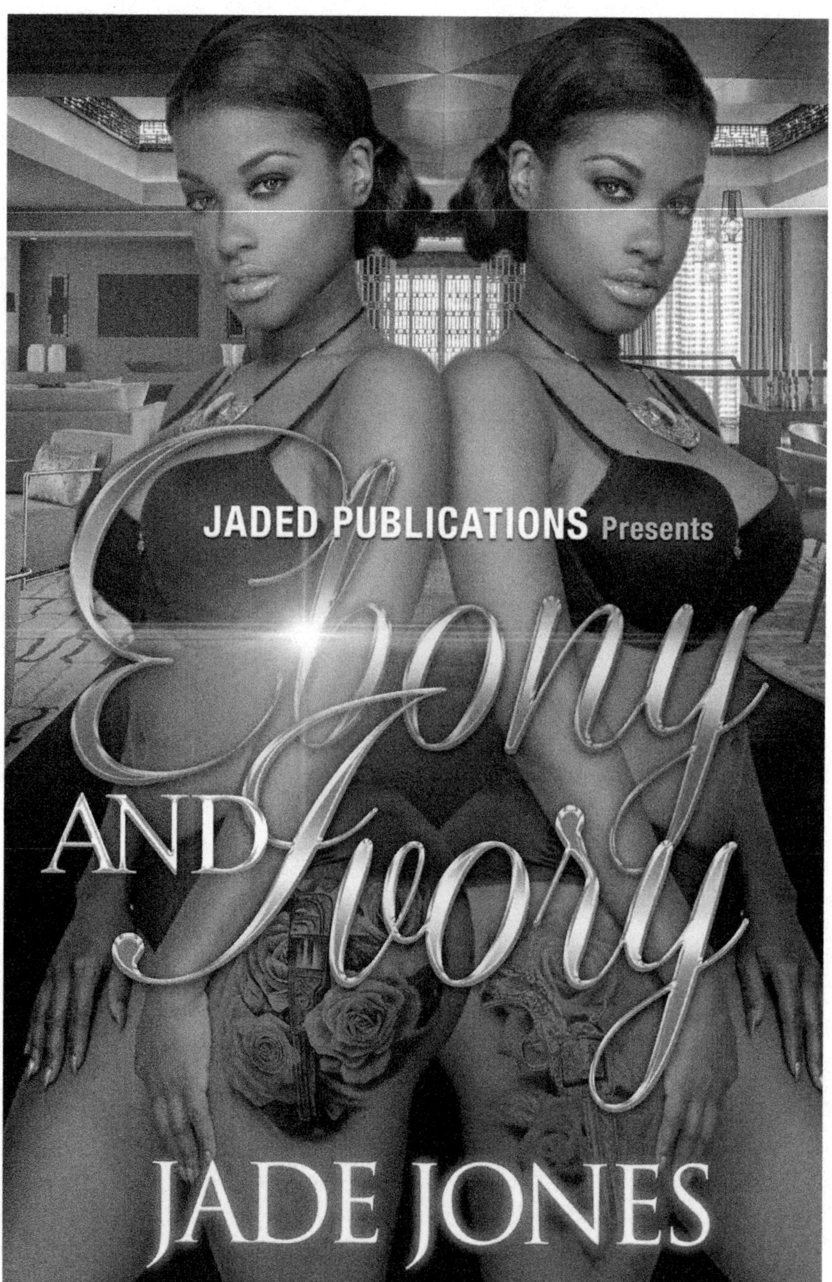
JADED PUBLICATIONS Presents
Ebony
AND Ivory
JADE JONES

JADED PUBLICATIONS Presents
Back Page
JADE JONES
&
CHASE MOORE

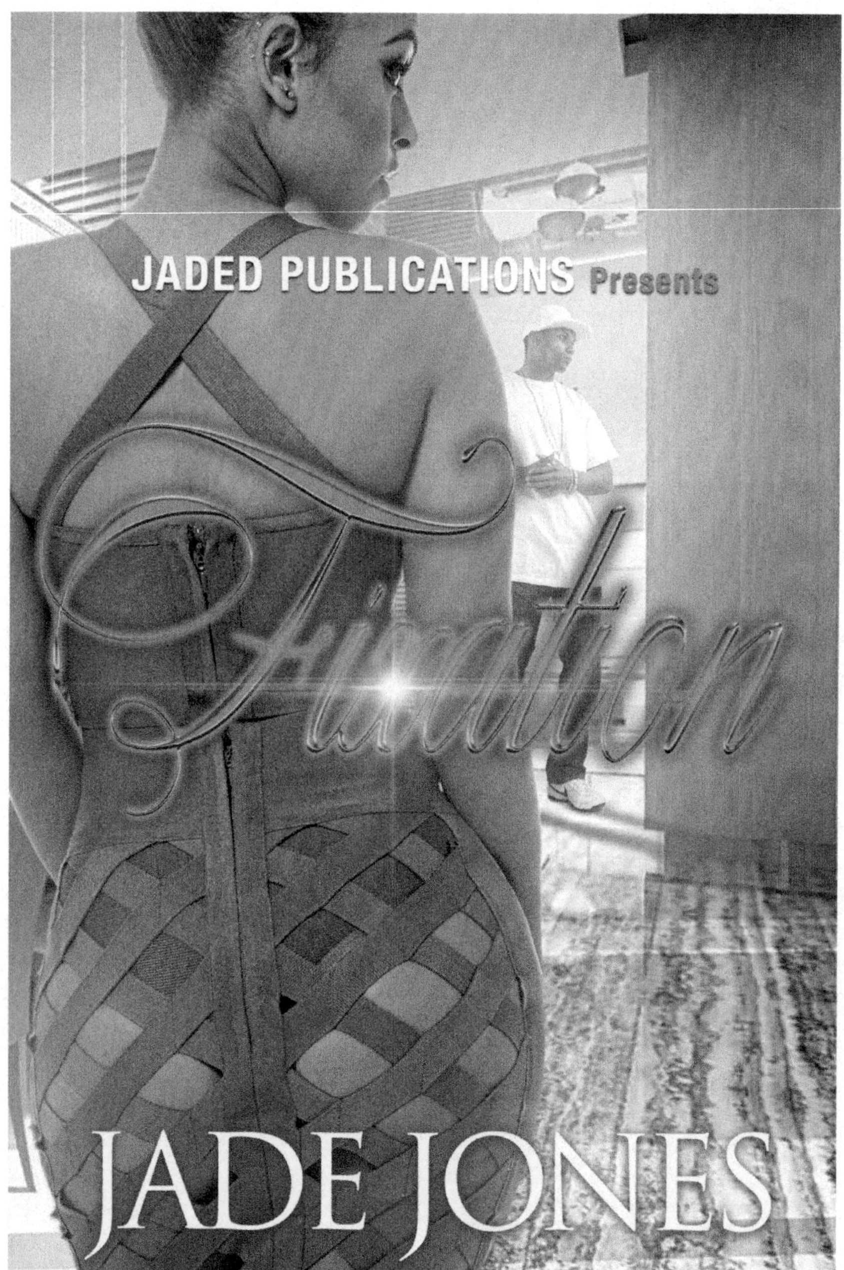
JADED PUBLICATIONS Presents
JADE JONES

JADED PUBLICATIONS Presents
PRETTY
Young
Things
CHASE MOORE

Made in the USA
Middletown, DE
23 June 2023

33334533R00146

Made in the USA
Middletown, DE
23 June 2023